"Don't reach out to people because they deserve it—do it for yourself."

Who was she to dole out unsolicited advice? She'd obviously confused herself with a self-help guru. And confused him with someone who cared. "Good night, Arianne."

He stepped off the curb.

"Gabe?"

Against his better judgment he turned. "Yes?" The single syllable held fourteen years of weariness.

She stood on her toes, sacrificing balance for height and letting herself stumble against him. His arms went around her ref̲_____ ̲laced a quick kiss j̲_____ ̲he'd turned his he̲_____ ̲ could have ca̲_____ away.

"Thank you for _____ ̲time," she said breathlessly.

Dear Reader,

I first "met" the character of Arianne Waide when I wrote her as a supporting role in a Christmas novella several years ago. She has always been fun to write and has made cameo appearances throughout my 4 SEASONS IN MISTLETOE series (often when giving her older brothers a piece of her mind). Readers have asked if she would have her own book, and I knew Arianne deserved to find love with a special, unforgettable hero!

In the close-knit community of Mistletoe, Georgia, Gabe Sloan is an outsider. His family history and a long-ago mistake have never truly allowed him to belong. When a tiny yet stubborn blonde good-naturedly bullies him into lending his time to a local fundraiser, Gabe decides to make this favor a farewell gesture. He's lived in Mistletoe without being a part of it for far too long, and he decides the best way to get closure from the past is to leave. But he didn't count on Arianne Waide's impulsive quest to help him mend fences with the town—and he certainly didn't count on falling for her.

Authors aren't supposed to have "favorite" characters from our books; we love them all, the same way moms appreciate their children's unique personalities. Still, I have to admit that Arianne and Gabe are very special to me. Whether this is your first visit to Mistletoe or your fourth, I hope you enjoy watching their story unfold.

Happy reading!

Tanya

Mistletoe Hero
TANYA MICHAELS

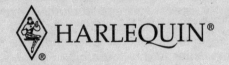

TORONTO • NEW YORK • LONDON
AMSTERDAM • PARIS • SYDNEY • HAMBURG
STOCKHOLM • ATHENS • TOKYO • MILAN • MADRID
PRAGUE • WARSAW • BUDAPEST • AUCKLAND

Recycling programs
for this product may
not exist in your area.

ISBN-13: 978-0-373-75283-6

MISTLETOE HERO

Copyright © 2009 by Tanya Michna.

www.eHarlequin.com

Printed in U.S.A.

ABOUT THE AUTHOR

Tanya Michaels began telling stories almost as soon as she could talk...and started stealing her mom's Harlequin romances less than a decade later. In 2003 Tanya was thrilled to have her first book, a romantic comedy, published by Harlequin Books. Since then, Tanya has sold nearly twenty books and is a two-time recipient of a Booksellers' Best Award as well as a finalist for the Holt Medallion, National Readers' Choice Award and Romance Writers of America's prestigious RITA® Award. Tanya lives in Georgia with her husband, two preschoolers and an unpredictable cat, but you can visit Tanya online at www.tanyamichaels.com.

Books by Tanya Michaels

HARLEQUIN AMERICAN ROMANCE

1170—TROUBLE IN TENNESSEE
1203—AN UNLIKELY MOMMY
1225—A DAD FOR HER TWINS
1235—MISTLETOE BABY*
1255—MISTLETOE CINDERELLA*
1270—MISTLETOE MOMMY*

HARLEQUIN TEMPTATION

 968—HERS FOR THE WEEKEND
 986—SHEER DECADENCE
1008—GOING ALL THE WAY

HARLEQUIN NEXT

DATING THE MRS. SMITHS
THE GOOD KIND OF CRAZY
MOTHERHOOD WITHOUT PAROLE

*4 Seasons in Mistletoe

For Jarrad. I love you.

Chapter One

"I vote you seduce him," Arianne Waide drawled.

"What?" Quinn Keller's shock came through the phone as clearly as if she'd been standing right there in the store. "Ari, I talked to the guy for ten seconds at the faculty welcome mixer, along with about sixty other people introducing themselves. He probably doesn't know I'm alive."

He would if you seduced him. But Arianne had only been teasing about that—it was a strategy she'd cultivated during her adolescence to deal with her parents and overprotective older brothers. Start with something outrageous first so that when you asked for what you really wanted, they were relieved to give it to you.

"All right, so not a full-fledged seduction," Arianne relented. "Why not just drop by his classroom tomorrow morning and ask if you can buy him lunch and answer any questions he has about the school or the town? Or, at the very least, recruit him to help you with the fall festival."

Silence stretched across the line as Quinn considered. "I could do that."

"Of course you could," Arianne encouraged.

"It's not that I'm shy," Quinn said, a touch defensively. "It's just…I'm so used to already knowing everyone in Mistletoe that I forget how to meet new people."

"I understand." *In theory.* Like Quinn, Arianne also grew up in the small north Georgia town of Mistletoe, but Arianne didn't have a bashful bone in her body. The youngest of three siblings, she'd learned early how to vie for attention and how to stick up for herself, often going toe-to-toe with her brother Tanner, who'd been the family prankster in his misspent youth.

Quinn sighed. "I should let you get back to work."

Arianne looked around the empty store her family had owned for three generations. Outside, parking lot lights reflected off the relentless drizzle that had made it such a chilly October day. "I promised Dad I'd finish the inventory report tonight, but I'm glad you called. This place is deserted. David bolted right at five so he could rush home and coo over the baby, and Dad's eating dinner with Mom and won't be back for another hour. I was getting tired of my own company."

Quinn laughed. "That's hard to imagine. Your company's always so…interesting."

"If I didn't know what a sweet woman you are, Quinn Keller, I'd have the sneaking suspicion I'd just been zinged."

"No comment."

"I'm hanging up on you now," Arianne said. "But promise you'll take my advice to heart?"

"I always do."

Quinn wasn't the only one. As Arianne put the phone back in its cradle, she indulged in a moment of self-satisfaction. She'd given romantic counsel to everyone from her older brothers to her brothers' wives to town pet-sitter Brenna Pierce. And she did so with enough confidence and wisdom that people listened, rarely questioning why they were taking suggestions from a woman who'd never actually had a serious relationship herself. She'd had opportunities, but had skirted any lasting, exclusive commitments.

The copper bell over the door jarred her from her thoughts and she turned with an automatic "Welcome to Waide Supply," even though she knew it was probably her father bringing takeout for her.

Nope. Her breath caught. Definitely not dear old dad. Instead, it was Gabe Sloan.

Her body trembled from the cool draft that swept inside, and she huddled deeper into her oversize cranberry sweater. "Hi."

Without breaking stride, Gabe nodded a hello in her direction, playing the strong, silent stereotype to the hilt. He was in here two or three times a week, but Arianne doubted he'd said a cumulative dozen words to her. Quinn characterized him as a mysterious loner. Having grown up with brothers, Arianne was less inclined to romanticize a guy.

Still, she had no trouble admitting that Gabe was

one sexy man. At least six feet tall, he was well-muscled from continuous hours of manual labor. He'd let his jet-black hair grow shaggy so that it tempted a woman to brush his bangs away from his clear gray eyes. Physically, everything about him invited contact: silky, collar-length hair just right for running your fingers through, broad shoulders that looked perfect for leaning against. His self-contained manner, however, projected a different message.

If Arianne had been busy with other customers, or if her brother and father were here with her, it would have been easier to ignore Gabe's presence. But the two of them alone on a rainy night created an almost intimate atmosphere. She put the inventory report on the counter in front of her, but couldn't help tracking Gabe down the aisle where hoses and spigots were kept.

Because shopping opportunities in Mistletoe were limited, Waide Supply provided a wide assortment of merchandise, serving as sort of a catch-all retailer for townspeople, but it was primarily a hardware store. Gabe, who earned his living as a self-employed handyman, was one of their best customers. As far as Arianne knew, he didn't advertise beyond a magnetic truck sign that read Sloan Carpentry and Odd Jobs. In Mistletoe, word of mouth went a long way, but still… Didn't the guy know how much a few well-applied business techniques could help him? The familiar urge to give unsolicited advice bubbled within her.

Smiling wryly, Arianne imagined his reaction. Somehow she doubted that Gabe was as persuadable as Quinn or even Arianne's stubborn father, Zachariah Waide. Then again, Arianne liked challenges. Her smile grew as she contemplated tactics. For starters, she had to engage him in actual conversation.

She got her chance when Gabe approached the counter with a few items that represented the variety of work he did—a coil of "soaker" hose, an adjustable wrench and a triangular-edged paintbrush. In flagrant disregard of the damp night, he wore a black T-shirt with no jacket.

Gazing appreciatively at his arms, she asked, "Aren't you cold?"

"No."

Progress! They'd moved from nonverbal gestures to a monosyllabic response.

Arianne rang up the hose on the cash register, then glanced toward the rain-streaked window. "Depressing weather. Has the rain been slowing down your work?" He had the natural, year-round tan of someone who worked outside on a near-daily basis.

"Not really." Rocking back on his heels, he regarded her with something like caution. It would probably look incongruous to an observer—a guy his size unnerved by her—but Arianne had grown accustomed to similar reactions from the men in her family.

She flashed him her most disarming grin and gave in to sheer impulse. "Gabe, would you like to have dinner with me sometime? Maybe this weekend?"

His jaw dropped, and Arianne experienced a rush of satisfaction. She'd penetrated that stoic exterior. How many women in Mistletoe could say the same?

But he'd already masked his surprise with a coolly assessing gaze beneath a raised eyebrow. "Dinner with you? Just how old are you, little girl?"

"Midtwenties. You do know that it's considered rude to ask a lady her age?" she asked playfully.

"Never claimed to be polite." Or playful apparently.

"So is this your way of turning down my dinner invitation?"

"Sorry. You aren't my type."

A less secure woman would be stung by this. She drew herself up to her full five-foot-two inches. "You don't like pretty blondes?"

Both his eyebrows went up this time; she'd caught him off guard again. His lips twitched, as if he might— wonder of wonders—smile. *Be still my beating heart.*

But his expression was annoyingly neutral when he replied, "Not really."

Arianne thought about telling him it was his loss, but that would be petty. When you asked someone on a date, you accepted refusal as a possibility and you were gracious about it. So she gave him a smile as sweet as her mama's peach cobbler and thrust his purchases at him. "You have a nice night, Gabe."

He hesitated as if uncertain he wanted to take the bag from her. "You, too." Then he left, the jangling bell punctuating his exit.

She watched him go. Arianne had caught herself watching him more frequently ever since this summer, when Quinn had hired Gabe to do some roofing repairs. As it turned out, seeing his muscular form while he dabbed away sweat with the hem of his T-shirt had been far different than Arianne's peripheral awareness of his being in the store while she was helping other customers. But what struck Arianne the most about Gabe wasn't his sculpted forearms or made-a-pact-with-the-devil abs. It was that she couldn't recall ever having seen him smile. His expression might have softened once or twice, when Quinn offered him something cold to drink or nervously tripped over her words, but a *real,* honest-to-goodness smile?

When the door opened again, Arianne whipped her head around, illogically expecting to see Gabe reappear.

"Brought you some dinner," Zachariah Waide said.

"Thanks, Dad." She sighed. "But you know you don't always have to come back for me. I'm just as capable as David of locking up the store by myself."

Her father frowned. "I don't like the idea of an attractive young woman being here late by herself. Especially when she's my daughter."

Arianne shook her head at his hypervigilance. This was *Mistletoe,* after all, hardly a hotbed of violent crime. The last time there'd been a… Abruptly she thought of the dark rumors once surrounding Gabe Sloan. Could they have anything to do with why she couldn't remember ever seeing him grin or hearing him laugh?

But that scandal was more than a decade ago. Then again, small towns had long memories.

Arianne found herself transported to that moment earlier when the corners of Gabe's eyes had crinkled and it had looked as if he might smile at her. For that heartbeat of time, she'd teetered on the edge of intoxicating potential. Coaxing a smile from him would be a victory on par with winning a critical play-off game.

And Arianne loved to win.

EXCLUDING PERIODIC PTA meetings and potluck church suppers, Wednesday nights in Mistletoe were not a flurry of social activity. During the summer, with kids out of school and tourists in town, the situation had been different, but when Gabe Sloan walked into On Tap now, he found the pool hall and local watering hole nearly empty. Aside from Nick Zeth throwing darts with a few firemen buddies and a lone couple circling lazily on the tiny dance floor, the only person present was the bartender.

Perfect. Gabe would be left alone without actually *being* alone.

"Usual?" the bartender asked.

"Yeah. Thanks." Gabe only ever ordered sodas, which he could have just as easily purchased at the Dixieland Diner on his way home. But the diner was too bright, too crowded, filled with chatty patrons and flirtatious waitresses he didn't want to encourage.

Had he done anything unintentional to encourage David Waide's little sister? Arianne. Gabe threw a couple of bills on the counter and reached for his soft drink, perplexed by the bizarre conversation back at the store. *"Would you like to have dinner with me?"* He wouldn't have been any more surprised if she'd announced that space aliens were landing on Main Street.

Until this evening, he and the youngest Waide had

barely spoken. So why on earth would she suddenly ask him out? Had she lost a bet? Was she trying to make another guy jealous?

His blood chilled at the stray possibility. He'd been a pawn in that particular game before, allowing himself to be manipulated when he was sixteen and stupid. Arianne had no doubt heard the story, even if it was an exaggerated version told by someone with no firsthand account of events. It made her offer even more bewildering. *Me and her?* She was the sunny only daughter of upstanding citizens, whereas Gabe's classmates his senior year had snickered and called him Gabriel the Angel of Death—though they'd snickered less audibly after the fistfight between him and Duke Allen.

Gabe couldn't imagine anyone who would make a more incongruous companion for him than Arianne. Before tonight, he hadn't given her appearance much thought, but she could be the poster child for wholesome cheer—fair-skinned, always smiling, with long wavy hair and big blue eyes. If he studied her closely, he might even have glimpsed a smattering of freckles above her pert nose. She looked like she should be having afternoon tea with Tinker Bell, not hitting on men nearly a foot taller than her.

Or was he reading too much into her overture? He frowned into his drink. Maybe her invitation hadn't been romantic in nature at all. Perhaps Arianne, whose family was well-known in Mistletoe and who had grown up among a throng of friends, simply felt sorry for him. Gabriel Sloan, outcast and sinner. He grimaced, the idea of her pity more distasteful than the idea of her romantic interest.

Normally Gabe shopped after sunset to make the most of daylight hours for his outside jobs, but he could change his schedule for a couple of weeks. If he'd been over at Waide Supply around noon, with more people in the store, Arianne wouldn't have singled him out. Gabe could—

Get a grip. Was he really planning to run from a five-foot blonde he could probably bench-press? No. Now that he'd refused her dinner invitation—rather bluntly, as a matter of fact—she'd probably prefer that they pretend it never happened.

Situation resolved.

Chapter Two

Arianne had grown up with no sisters and was ecstatic that she now had two. It was great to see both her brothers happily wed, especially since she thoroughly approved of the women they'd chosen to marry. Currently Arianne sat on the floor of Lilah Waide's living room. While David and Rachel Waide, proud parents of three-and-a-half-month-old Bailey, lived in a suburb closer to downtown Mistletoe, Tanner and Lilah lived in a gorgeous, oversize cottage-style home they'd built on the outskirts of town. Lilah said that her favorite parts of the day were the twenty-five-minute ride to and from Whiteberry Elementary; Tanner drove her and picked her up, so they had time at the beginning and end of each day to make each other laugh or privately vent frustrations.

"All right." Seated on the couch, looking every bit the elementary school teacher with reading glasses perched on the end of her nose, Lilah tapped her pen on the clipboard she held. "Let's look at the preparations, figure out where the gaping holes are and try to spackle them in."

The repair metaphor made Arianne think of Gabe. And last night's encounter. If she'd used a more subtle approach, might he have accepted her invitation? Not that it mattered—Ari didn't do subtle.

Curled comfortably in a wicker-framed papasan chair that faced the huge back-wall window, fall festival cochair Quinn consulted her own clipboard. "Food is covered. Pete and Vonda and a few of their friends from the senior center are going to run the bingo tent for us. Vonda already went around town, getting people to donate prizes."

Arianne laughed at that. "She probably terrorized them until they gave her whatever she wanted." It was impossible to say no to the fiery seventysomething who, like Arianne and Quinn, had been a bridesmaid at Lilah's wedding last winter. Arianne adored the elderly woman.

Lilah read from her list. "We have some kids from the high school taking care of music for us, and a lot of moms have volunteered this year. The difficult part will be organizing them all. The Kerrigans are setting up the tables and coordinating the judges for the jack-o-lantern contest. Brenna and Adam promised to be in charge of face-painting. Ari, can we put you down to work the kissing booth?"

"Sure, why not? It's for a good cause." Most of the guys in Mistletoe were harmless. They'd donate their dollar to the school and give her a quick peck before disappearing into the festival crowd to try their hand at a skill game or purchase food. The fact that Arianne had two looming brothers—who had apparently used up all the good height genes in her family—dissuaded any wiseacres from trying anything inappropriate at the booth.

Every year, Whiteberry Elementary, where both Quinn and Lilah taught, hosted a fall festival fundraiser. They held it downtown because the parking at the school itself was too limited, and local businesses helped sponsor the activities. Quinn and Lilah had agreed to cochair this year's festival committee. They'd somehow dragged Arianne and their mutual friend Brenna Pierce along for the ride, although neither of them worked for the school or had kids enrolled there. Brenna, however, had been excused from this afternoon's meeting. By Thanksgiving, her work schedule would be jam-packed with holiday pet-sitting, so she was taking advantage of a quiet few days now to go with her boyfriend to Tennessee and visit his three kids.

"Honestly," Lilah said as she scanned her sheet, "we have the majority of it covered. But there are some minor construction and wiring issues we'll need help with. I've already drafted Tanner. I wish we had more active dads in my class this year. The mothers are great help when it comes to the bake sale and signing up for story circle, but there aren't many who are comfortable with power tools. Or capable of heavy lifting. We're shorthanded on muscle this year, especially since the PE coach broke his arm last weekend."

"I don't know what he was thinking." Quinn shook her head. "A man his age jumping at a skateboard park!"

Arianne pinned Quinn with a gaze. "Weren't you

supposed to be getting us more muscle, in the form of the cute new teacher Mr. Flannery?"

Quinn held up her hands. "I will, I swear. I just didn't have the opportunity yet. He was out today with the stomach bug that's been going around the classes."

"Patrick Flannery?" Lilah grinned. "He *is* cute. Maybe you should take him some soup and well-wishes."

"Nah," Arianne said. "You can do the well-wishes over the phone without risking germs. Plus, if you ask him for a favor when he's feverish, he may agree simply because he's too delirious to come up with an excuse."

"Machiavellian," Quinn said with admiration. "I bet *you* can get a guy to agree to anything!"

"Not so. Just last night…" It occurred to Arianne that maybe she didn't want to share the story of how Gabe Sloan had shot her down. Not because she was embarrassed—it wasn't that big a deal—but because her friends might read too much into it. "Hey, why am I the only one without a clipboard here? I feel cheated."

Lilah rolled her eyes at the non sequitur. "Fess up, Waide. We want the rest of the story."

"I asked Gabe Sloan if he wanted to have dinner with me," Ari admitted as casually as she could.

It was a good thing *she* had perspective on the matter. The same could not be said for her friends. Lilah's eyes doubled in diameter, and Quinn flopped back in her chair so hard the wicker base wobbled.

"Gabriel Sloan!" they chorused. It was hard to tell whether they were appalled or delighted. They definitely weren't nonchalant.

"Oh, fine." Ari sighed. "Get it all out of your systems. Anyone want to gush about how dreamy he is? Someone prank dial him while I doodle our names together in a heart on my clipboard. Oh, wait, I don't have one."

Lilah reached down to smack Ari lightly on the back of the head. "I can't believe you didn't tell me you were interested in him. Do your brothers know about this?"

Before Ari could explain that this had been a onetime invitation, not serious interest, Quinn protested, "It's not like she kept it a secret. She's been commenting since summer how sexy he is."

"I do recall mentioning that a couple of times," Arianne admitted. And who could blame her? No one in town disputed his quietly wicked appeal—it was part of the basis of the scandal. Although, personally, Arianne felt Shay Templeton was more than equally to blame. Few ever voiced that opinion, though. Probably out of respect for the dead.

"So why did he turn you down?" Lilah asked, dragging Arianne back to the present.

"Said something about my not being his type."

The other two women looked outraged, talking over top of each other in their haste to stick up for her.

"But you're—"

"A Waide! Everyone in this town—"

"Beautiful. I couldn't get *my* hair to look like that—"

"—loves you. Who does he thinks he is?"

"Is he blind?"

Arianne giggled. "Well, thanks for the outpouring of

support, but I wasn't losing sleep over it. Maybe I'm really not his type. He's entitled to feel that way."

"Huh." Quinn rocked back in her chair, thoughtful. "For a guy who looks like a walking magnet for any female with a pulse, I can't remember the last time I heard he was dating anyone. What do you suppose his type is?"

They were all silent for a moment, and Arianne wondered if her friends were also thinking about Shay Templeton. *God, she would have been about my age when she died.* Arianne was sure that, at some point in her childhood, she'd seen the woman, but she'd never had real reason to take notice.

Ari looked at Lilah, the oldest of the three of them. "Do you think the story is true?"

Lilah shrugged. "Depends on which version you mean."

The Templetons had been a wealthy, tempestuous couple, known for loud fights in the dining room of the country club. One valet reported stumbling across them while they passionately made up in their parked car. Mr. Templeton had been nearly forty, a decade and a half older than his wife, and devoted to the law firm in which he was partner. Gossip ran that whenever Shay got to feeling neglected, she would shower affection on a chosen young man, playing to Templeton's one insecurity to provoke his jealous attention. But, as far as Arianne knew, none of the men she'd flirted with had been as young as sixteen-year-old lawn boy Gabe Sloan. One story had Gabe shooting Mr. Templeton in a jealous rage, with Shay falling down the curved staircase to her death as she and her lover tried to flee. Other citizens scoffed that Gabe wasn't even at the house at the time the gunshot was reported. The end result remained the same—Shay Templeton had a broken neck and Mr. Templeton had been shot with his own revolver.

It was rare for something so controversial to happen here in Mistletoe, and the whole sordid tale had grown into local legend. *Making Gabe some sort of cross between Don Juan and a yeti.*

"Why do you think he's stayed all these years?" Arianne asked. She knew Gabe's father still lived in Mistletoe, but she didn't think she'd ever seen them together publicly. Were they close?

"Whatever the truth is, it's a sad story." Quinn rolled her shoulders back as if trying to shrug off impending gloom. "What made you ask him out, Ari?"

"Don't know, really. Like you said, I've noticed how attractive he was. This just happened to be the first time I found myself alone with him. Why *not* ask him out? It's how I'd approach any other guy who interested me."

Lilah and Quinn shot her pointed looks. Gabe Sloan was so not "any other guy." He was in a category unto himself.

"Will it be awkward next time he comes into the store?" Quinn asked. "That's one of the reasons I'm hesitant about Patrick, or any man associated with the school. I have to be there every day, cheerful and patient for the kids, I can't risk creating an uncomfortable work environment."

"I don't feel awkward about his rejection at all," Ari

insisted. "And I can prove it. You guys say we need some extra muscle to help with the festival? I know just the solution."

Her friends gaped at her as if she'd lost her ever-loving mind.

"What? Haven't you *seen* his biceps?" she demanded. "The festival is a community tradition. He's part of the community."

"Not in the strictest sense," Lilah argued gently.

"Then, maybe it's time he was." Arianne's natural determination had kicked in; there was little chance of anyone dissuading her now.

She thought of her large, close-knit family and the warm, nurturing sanctuary Mistletoe had always been for her. It pained her to think of her comforting hometown being something more sinister for Gabe. For whatever reason, he'd chosen to stay—maybe because of his family ties or maybe just because he, like her, was a stubborn cuss, refusing to be driven out by furtive speculation.

Whatever the reason, if he planned to remain, it only made sense that he'd eventually want to perform a role in their shared society besides supporting player in a fourteen-year-old tragedy.

Ari brightened. She'd been feeling a bit melancholy lately as the golden summer days shortened into the early darkness of fall. It was probably just the natural letdown now that all the activity surrounding Lilah's wedding—Ari had been the maid of honor—and preparations for Rachel's baby—Ari had helped repaint the nursery and had been the backup Lamaze coach—were behind them. For almost two years, it seemed as if her family had been frenzied with events, and she suddenly found herself at loose ends as she watched her brothers move on with their lives. They no longer needed her advice and help. But perhaps she'd stumbled across a new challenge worthy of her considerable energy.

Gabe Sloan didn't know how lucky he was.

Chapter Three

"Hi. Mind if I sit here?"

Gabe choked on a bite of his pulled-pork sandwich. Where the devil had *she* come from? Glancing at Arianne Waide's pixie features, he speculated that perhaps she'd used fairy dust to simply materialize here.

Before he could answer that he did mind—and that there were at least half a dozen unoccupied tables nearby—Arianne sat on the wooden bench opposite him. She impatiently moved aside the tabletop roll of paper towel between them. The restaurant didn't boast impressive interior decor, but the barbecue was phenomenal.

If Gabe were a better person, he'd think it was a shame more people didn't know about this hidden treasure. By all rights, it should be just as crowded as the Dixieland Diner. But he was selfishly glad he never had to wait in a long line during the lunch hour and that he wasn't jostling elbows with locals like Arianne.

"I've come to ask you a favor," she declared.

"What is wrong with you?" This time he knew he

hadn't done anything to encourage her attention. So what was she doing stalking him to the far side of town at his favorite hole-in-the-wall?

"Careful." She wagged her index finger at him. "Last time we spoke, your manners were a bit rough, but I'm willing to overlook that and start fresh."

"How nice." Was she deranged? The explanation seemed likelier with each passing moment. "To what do I owe this magnanimous oversight?" Whatever he'd done to earn it, he'd make sure not to repeat.

"I'm naturally kindhearted," she drawled.

Looking alarmingly as if she were settling in for a prolonged conversation, Arianne propped her elbows on the table and rested her cheek on her fists. It was the kind of posture that should have appeared youthful. Except that when she brought her arms together like that, it pushed together a surprising amount of cleavage in the scooped neckline of her fuzzy green sweater. He couldn't recall what she'd been wearing Wednesday night, but he was sure it had been looser. And that it hadn't seemed so damn touchable. Annoyed that he'd even noticed, he clenched his fingers into a fist on his thigh.

In spite of her small stature and wavy locks, she was definitely all woman. *A woman whose company I didn't ask for.*

"Look, kid, I'm *not* kindhearted. I'm an ill-tempered misanthrope. Fancy word for someone who doesn't like people."

Most females would get huffy over his condescension and implied aspersions on their maturity. Arianne widened her smile.

"I understand," she assured him. There was so much commiserating sincerity in her tone that it took him a moment to realize she was reflecting his patronization right back at him. "You're a genuine ogre. Probably live in a swamp, hang out with a talking donkey—"

"You have an odd strategy for asking favors," he informed her as he stood.

"You're leaving?" She shot an incredulous glance toward his plate, which still held most of his onion rings, the last quarter of his sandwich and a pickle spear.

"Lost my appetite."

"In that case." She reached unabashedly for an onion ring, closing her eyes and making a near-purring sound in her throat. Once she'd swallowed, she beamed at him in approval. "Wow, those are good."

"I know."

"Why don't I eat here more?" she wondered aloud, popping another hand-battered onion ring into her mouth. With a final resigned glance at the food, she stood, too.

Gabe had the terrible suspicion that she'd fall in step with him and trail him wherever he went. That if he went to the parking lot and drove away, she might actually follow; if he tried to evade her by going into the men's room, she'd simply wait him out. He doubted he could squeeze through the window.

"I should have been clearer earlier," she said, her voice suddenly brisk and businesslike. "When I said I came to ask a favor, that was true, but it's not just how you can help me, it's how we can help each other."

The old cynicism burned in his gut. If she suggested in husky tones that she could scratch his back if he scratched hers, he would lose all respect for her. And it startled Gabe to realize that even though he barely knew her and had spent the majority of this encounter wishing she'd disappear in a puff of smoke, he did respect her. She had an…implacability that was commendable.

That slight admiration kept him from telling her point-blank to get lost. Instead, he crossed his arms over his chest. "I have a busy afternoon ahead of me—we don't all work for our daddies. You have thirty seconds."

"You remember Quinn Keller, the teacher who hired you to repair her roof last June?"

He nodded. Quinn was a decent sort. She'd tipped him for the work he'd done without winking over the check as though he was supposed to add some extra service—something more than one town matron had hinted in his younger years. Quinn would bring out freshly squeezed lemonade on hot days but seemed unnerved enough by him that she kept their conversations brief.

Unlike certain blondes who seemed determined to chat him up from now until the Second Coming.

The moment he'd inclined his head, Arianne hurriedly continued as if mentally counting down the time he'd allotted her. "Quinn's cochairing the committee for Whiteberry's fall festival and needs help with some of the labor—assembling booths, hooking up electrical equipment—but she doesn't have much of a budget. After all, the whole point is to raise money for the school. So we wanted to ask you to do it for free."

He snorted. The lady had a bottomless supply of gall. "And I'd be doing this out of the nonexistent goodness of my heart? You have a nice day, Miss Waide."

He headed for the door with a deliberately long stride, but what she lacked in long legs she made up for in unholy tenacity. No sooner had he stepped into the cool afternoon air than that voice once again sounded at his ear—or rather, six inches below it. With her non-stop chirping, he would have expected her to have a shrill tone or maybe something nasal, with a hint of whine. She actually had a low, melodic pitch. It wasn't hard to imagine that she'd used that voice to convince plenty of people to do her bidding.

"Gabe," she chided, "don't you think it's silly to run away? It's not like you can hide from me in a town this size."

She had a point. After all, he periodically crossed paths with Shay's parents and heaven knew they weren't actively seeking him out the way Arianne was threatening. "No reason to hide when I can outdistance you, short stuff."

"You can try. I'll get a scooter and keep up. Ask my brothers if you don't believe me."

Oh, he did. He just wasn't sure how he'd become the object of her persistence. For months she'd simply been the checkout girl at the most reliable place in town to get hardware supplies. Then she'd dropped that bombshell of a dinner date on him, and suddenly he had a smiling thorn in his side who smelled like raspberries.

"Miss Waide, just so we're clear, you know I was serious when I said you weren't my type? I'm not playing hard to get or something."

For a moment, her blue eyes glinted, darkening with some unnamed emotion. Had he angered her? Hurt her?

He refused to feel bad, not if the end result was her staying away from him. In the long run, he'd be doing her a favor.

Her tone cooled. "My proposition today wasn't of a romantic nature, trust me. Let's just forget about the other night. It was an isolated incident, prompted solely by—by…" Here she stumbled.

Without meaning to, he took a step closer to her. "Yes? Why *did* you ask me out?"

"Well." She squared her shoulders, trying to look as composed as she had been inside the barbecue house. Yet the pulse in the hollow of her throat beat more rapidly. She reflexively licked her lips, a movement that might have seemed calculated in another woman, but seemed like genuine nervousness in Arianne's case. "You're an attractive man, and I'm an attractive woman. Dinner together didn't seem that crazy when I suggested it."

An attractive man. For years, women—those his own age to those slightly younger on up to those far older who should know better—had looked at him as if, on the outside, he was near flawless. Inside he was a mess, but too few seemed to care about that.

"You think you're attractive?" He gave Arianne a

deliberate once-over, letting his gaze slowly drop down her body.

She swallowed, standing stock-still as the wind whipped her hair around her face. "You're trying to intimidate me."

"It's working. And it's probably a lesson you need. Bite-size morsels like you shouldn't chase after the big bad wolf."

She surprised him by taking a sudden step forward, nearly erasing the remaining gap between them. "I grew up with two older brothers who taught me not to back down in the face of bullies, so save your bluster for someone else. I don't think you're that big or that bad."

You're wrong. But her clear gaze was so piercing that for a second he almost couldn't find his voice. "Arianne, you're a Mistletoe native. I know you've... Whatever you've heard about me, it's probably true."

It was a minor victory that she looked away first.

But she regrouped, meeting his eyes as she asked softly, "Why do you stay?"

He stiffened. "None of your damn business."

"Because if you feel like you, I don't know, maybe owe something to—"

"Drop it." The words came out in a low growl.

Her eyes widened and, for a change, she listened. She kept her mouth shut as he crossed the few feet of asphalt from where he'd stood to his truck.

He should've known it was too good to last.

"Will you at least think about helping with the festival? For the good of the town?" she implored.

"No." He unlocked his door.

"How about this?" She played her ace. "You help Quinn slap together a couple of booths, and I promise never to disturb you again."

When you put it like that... Feeling unfairly beleaguered and somehow years older than when he'd arrived for lunch half an hour ago, he slapped his hand on the side of the truck and looked back at her.

Arianne offered him a beatific smile.

Against his better judgment, he heard himself say, "I'll think about it."

SUNDAYS WERE THE ONLY DAY of the week Gabe didn't work, so it was the perfect time to catch up on mundane errands. *Like grocery shopping.* Surveying his barren kitchen pantry, he mentally cursed himself for not remembering to pick up coffee sooner. He debated whether there was enough left to make a full two cups, then opted instead for one really strong mug to kick-start his morning.

Twenty minutes later, he got in the pickup truck and headed for town. There was only one main grocery store in Mistletoe, and it had a huge parking lot to accommodate as many citizens as possible. Right now the lot was nearly empty. Most people were either taking advantage of the weekend to sleep in or at church.

Gabe had once considered visiting one of the town's houses of worship, wondering if he could find...what, redemption? But he'd decided to spare both himself and the good folks of Mistletoe the discomfort. Shay's parents were both Sunday school teachers at the Baptist church; the Methodist church was where Gabe's own parents had been married. He'd been told his mother had been a soprano in the choir, and as a boy, Gabe had liked to imagine she'd once sung to him, even though there'd been little more than a week between his birth and her death.

He grabbed a cart on the sidewalk and propelled it toward the automatic entrance doors. *First stop, coffee aisle.* Moving purposely through the store, he piled staples into the cart: ground beans, filters, steaks, juice, cereal, new razor blades, eggs and cheese. He was en route to the freezers and his one major vice—besides coffee, of course—when he had the unpleasant prickling sensation of being watched. Slowly he turned, half expecting Arianne Waide to wave at him from a soft drink display. If that were the case, he vowed he'd put an end once and for all to—

His stomach tightened, then dropped about ten feet. "Sir." Gabe swallowed, hating the arctic glare of Jeremy Sloan's pale eyes, but unable to look away.

What is he doing here? Gabe's father should have been in some congregation pew among his righteous brethren, not skulking the aisles of the Mistletoe Mart.

"Gabriel." The older man spoke without the banked anger Gabe remembered. Instead his tone was flat.

Gabe floundered for a response.

How've you been, Pops?

I see you're eating the same brand of cereal after all these years.

Still hate me?

Gabe had shifted his gaze to the contents of his father's cart because it seemed far more innocuous than looking at the man who'd dutifully raised him but never warmed to him. Yet now that Gabe took a closer look, the groceries he saw sent a ripple of foreboding through him. Cereal, a large can of coffee, some ground round, dairy, orange juice and shaving supplies. *So what? We both drink coffee and eat red meat. I'm nothing like him.*

Not in the ways that mattered anyway. Their physical, superficial resemblances were undeniable. The same icy eyes, too devoid of color to be called blue; the same tall, muscular frames. Though Jeremy was fast approaching sixty—and showed it in every bitter line on his face—he was undoubtedly stronger than a lot of men in their forties.

Jeremy cleared his throat. "Need to get this milk and cheese home. Into the fridge."

Gabe nodded, feeling both relief and anger when his father turned to go. But the anger was more of a remembered, phantom emotion—a holdover from the past—than what he was experiencing now. The truth was, encounters with his own parent were in some ways more painful than the times Gabe ran into Shay's parents. Gabe was grateful the awkward moment had passed so quickly.

He progressed to the frozen-foods section and grabbed a gallon of Breckfield Banana Crème ice cream. With effort he managed not to look over his shoulder. *Even if he caught you buying it, so what?*

Gabe was no longer a child who could be scolded for smuggling sweets into the house.

I don't want to see you dishonoring your mother's memory by eating that sugary garbage, boy. Diabetes is hereditary.

Beth Ann Sloan's diabetes had fatally complicated her post-Cesarean infection. Gabe had grown up unsure whether his father blamed the disease or the baby who'd been brought into the world from that C-section.

A surge of negative emotions rose in him, and Gabe added a half gallon of chocolate ice cream to his buggy. He was reaching for a pint of home-style vanilla when he stopped himself with a sigh. Was he going to let seeing his father reduce him to the level of a rebellious twelve-year-old, or finally grow a pair and decide not to care that his own flesh and blood couldn't stand the sight of him?

He put back the chocolate and moved on to the next row.

Moving on. Now there was an idea. It wouldn't have to be fleeing Mistletoe with his tail tucked between his legs—no one's opinion here mattered enough to run him out of town—but simply leaving for a fresh start. As early as middle school, he'd started dreaming of college. Going somewhere, *any*where, away from his father.

Arianne Waide appeared in his mind just as abruptly as she'd materialized at the barbecue house earlier this week. *Why do you stay?* she'd asked. Good question. Granted, college scholarships had ceased to be an option after the deaths of Shay and Roger Templeton. Gabe had graduated by the skin of his teeth, but high school had been a long time ago.

Gabe told himself that he didn't care about the past. Could he let himself care about a future?

Chapter Four

"I hate to say this because you'll probably let it go to your head," Quinn teased, "but your advice was absolutely spot-on."

"That's because I'm wise beyond my years." In the crowded lot outside the Dixieland Diner, Arianne narrowly squeezed her car into a space between an oversize truck and a sedan that had parked crookedly. "I should run for mayor."

Quinn unfastened her seat belt with a chuckle. "This is sort of what I meant by letting it go to your head."

Meeting for Sunday brunch was a semiregular tradition for the two friends, and Arianne had known as soon as she'd seen the other woman's bright smile that Quinn had finally talked to Patrick Flannery. On the drive to the diner, Quinn had said he'd agreed to help with the festival; he'd even admitted that he'd been looking for a way to get more involved and meet people in the community but hadn't known where to start. Quinn had casually mentioned that they could discuss the festival more over dinner this week.

As they got out of the car, Arianne asked, "So are you grateful enough for my suggestion that you're buying?"

"On a teacher's salary?" Quinn snorted. "Dream on."

"When I become mayor, I'll see what I can do about getting you guys pay raises."

"I'd laugh, except part of me thinks you'll actually run someday and probably talk me into being your campaign manager."

Grinning, Arianne turned to look at her friend, but she forgot what she was going to say when she noticed the red pickup truck driving past the diner. *Gabe.* Her heart beat faster, and she had one of those annoying flashback moments she'd been experiencing for the past few days. In random moments—as she drifted to sleep, or when the shop bell rang and she thought it might be him coming into the store—she would relive their last conversation, when they'd been toe-to-toe and she could feel the heat coming off his body. When she'd been deliciously uncertain whether he'd been about to shake her or kiss her.

All right, that last part might have been a fanciful embellishment. Gabe showed no signs of wanting to kiss her, and he was too aloof to shake anyone. If he'd once been swept away with passion over a married woman, he'd learned from his mistakes.

Quinn followed her gaze. "Isn't that—"

A squeal of tires interrupted her question. Although the pickup hadn't been going that fast, Gabe had apparently decided at the last minute to make the left-hand turn.

"He's coming toward us," Quinn whispered.

Arianne nodded, watching wide-eyed as he navigated the crowded parking lot and finally rolled to a stop a few feet away from them.

He crooked his finger out the open window and beckoned toward them. Under other circumstances, Arianne might have scoffed that she wasn't the type who could be summoned like that, but there was no chance she would deny her raging curiosity. Both women exchanged puzzled glances and walked forward.

After Arianne's last meeting with Gabe, he'd seemed more likely to peel out in the opposite direction than pursue her. Unless he'd deduced her plans to follow up with him later in the week and was making a preemptive strike, she couldn't imagine what he wanted to discuss.

"Hi, Quinn." Gabe called out a relaxed greeting that ignored Arianne entirely. Except that his gaze was locked with hers.

"H-hi."

He continued in that same easy tone that didn't match the banked intensity of his eyes. "Your friend tells me that you could use a hand. With the fair."

Quinn couldn't quite mask her surprise; Arianne didn't bother trying. Her mouth fell open. She'd planned to wear him down, but she hadn't expected it to happen so quickly. *Damn, I'm good.*

"That's right," Quinn said. "The fair's October 24, and we would appreciate any help you can give us getting ready."

"Two weeks," Gabe muttered, almost to himself. Then he nodded. "I should be able to make that work."

Make it work? Was he still talking about the festival?

Recalling the times her mom had used a good meal to coax conversation from reluctant men, Arianne invited, "Why don't you join us for breakfast and we can talk about the fair some more?"

"No. Thank you," he added with a polite nod toward Quinn. "Got groceries in the back."

"We won't keep you then," Quinn said.

Speak for yourself. "Quinn, would you mind putting our names down for a table? I'll be there in just a second," Arianne promised.

Quinn nodded without hesitation, but Arianne knew her friend would be full of questions once they were alone. As soon as Quinn walked away, Arianne's gaze snapped back to Gabe, his pull on her practically tangible. She sighed inwardly. *Why are the hot ones emotionally unavailable?*

"I'm glad you've changed your mind about the fair," she said. "When did you decide to help?"

"About three minutes ago," he said. "I was on my way home, thinking about something you said the other day."

"Yeah?" She went tingly and warm with pride.

He stared through his windshield. "You asked why I stayed."

She'd suggested that maybe he felt, deep down, as if he owed something to the town. Maybe he was ready to extend an olive branch. Naturally Arianne would help. It was far past time for Gabe Sloan and the citizens of Mistletoe to—

"So I'm leaving," he said on an exhale.

"What?"

He nodded, his expression calm and inching closer to happy than she'd ever seen. Even if he still hadn't smiled.

"I'll help with this fair—why not? It'll be like my parting gift," he said wryly. "And then I'm getting the hell out of Dodge."

"SO WHAT'S THIS I HEAR about Gabe Sloan trying to run down my sister in the Dixieland parking lot?" Tanner Waide mock-growled as he stepped inside the supply store on Monday morning.

Arianne paused in the act of stocking the register drawer with bills and coins, glancing toward the door that led to the private office in back. "Shh! You know better than to make dumb comments like that with Mr. Overprotective on the premises."

Tanner approached the counter, chuckling. "Please. You actively seek out opportunities to provoke Dad into worrying so that you can argue with him about how capable you are."

"Hey." She shot him an indignant look. "You forget, I *matured* during the years you were away from Mistletoe. I don't intentionally pick fights." Sometimes they just happened to occur in her vicinity, usually because others were having a hard time seeing reason.

Her older brother raised an eyebrow, skeptical.

"Did you stop by just to harass me?" she wanted to know.

"No, I promised David I'd come by to go over some first-quarter projections." Although Tanner, who'd formerly worked as a financial bigwig in Atlanta, wasn't a full-time employee of the family store, he did help with their books.

"David's running late," Arianne said. "Apparently the baby had a very fussy night."

Tanner set down his briefcase. "Guess I'll have a cup of coffee while I wait and harass you after all. So…anything going on between you and Gabe Sloan?"

"Yes, I asked him to help set up the fall festival and he agreed." She rolled her eyes. "It's all very tantalizing. Are people still so suspicious of him that they're paying attention to his every conversation? Because we spoke at a public place in broad daylight. I can't imagine that makes for very interesting gossip."

Cocking his head to the side, Tanner regarded her thoughtfully. "Actually, I heard about it when I ran into Shane McIntyre at the gas station this morning, and I'm pretty sure his interest was in *you,* not Sloan—but your wildly defensive attitude is intriguing."

"Oh." She looked down, not sure what to say. *Maybe it would be better to keep your mouth shut for a change of pace.*

"It's funny," Tanner added, "but when you got angry about people being 'suspicious' of him, you sounded almost as overprotective as you accuse Dad of being."

Could Gabe use someone to speak up in his defense? Her parents had tried to shield her young ears from the initial gossip, so other than being peripherally aware of the Templetons' deaths and Gabe's rumored connection, Arianne was vague on details. Who had Gabe been friends with when he was in high school? Had anyone stuck up for him? Had Mr. Sloan tried to shield his only child?

"Ari?"

"Sorry, not a morning person." She pointed toward the back office. "Better bring me some of that coffee, too."

He gave her a knowing, lopsided grin. "Was that your way of dismissing me?"

"I always said you were the smart brother."

"What's that make me?" David asked, once the copper bell above the door had heralded his arrival. "The good-looking one?"

Tanner snorted. "Out of sympathy for your rough night, I won't even point out how ridiculous that statement is."

As their older sibling got closer, Arianne saw just how uncharacteristically rumpled he was. David had tucked his wrinkled shirt into khaki slacks but had forgotten his belt. His brown hair, while still shorter than Tanner's, had outgrown its normal cut and there were dark circles under his Waide-blue eyes. But even the lines of fatigue on his face couldn't erase his obvious joy at being a parent.

"Got new pictures of my niece?" Arianne asked. It had become their morning ritual.

He tossed her his cell phone, which she caught one-handed. "Took one right before I left. She looked… *Angelic* is the only word for it."

Studying the photo on the small screen, Arianne had to agree. Still, she laughed at his assessment. "Angelic? That would be the same child who cried all night?"

"Not her fault," the proud papa insisted. "She's cut-ting her first teeth. We tried everything mentioned in Rach's parenting books, but none of the solutions worked for very long."

"You want me to stop by this afternoon?" Arianne offered. "Give Rachel a break, or at least a hand?"

"Thank you." David tousled her hair affectionately. "For that, I'm willing to overlook that you called *this* bonehead 'the smart brother.'"

"Don't take that personally," Tanner said. "She was only sucking up to me to distract me from asking about Gabe Sloan."

"Gabe Sloan?" David narrowed his eyes at Arianne. "What's going on with you and Sloan?"

"Nothing! As I already explained to Tanner."

The two men exchanged irritatingly brotherly glances. Then, in unison, they swiveled their gazes back to her.

She sighed in exasperation. "All right, you caught me. Last week, I sold him some soaker hose, and yesterday he said he'd help Quinn and Lilah with their festival preparations."

And, in between, she also might have stalked him at a barbecue house, but why bore her brothers with every minuscule detail of her personal life? The gist was sufficient.

Tanner held up his hands in defeat. "Obviously Shane read too much into yesterday's encounter. He said that Sloan seemed anxious to talk to you and you looked—"

The door on the far side of the store creaked open, and their father smiled at them, counteracting his gruff tone when he demanded, "Am I paying the three of you to stand around yakking?"

"Sorry, Dad," Tanner said cheerfully. "We got preoccupied quizzing Ari about who she's dating."

Zachariah Waide zeroed in on his daughter. "You're seeing someone?"

"You'd better sleep with one eye open," she muttered in Tanner's direction.

He laughed. "Luckily Lilah's a light sleeper. She'll protect me."

Arianne walked around the edge of the counter. "I am going to get my coffee now. Ya'll don't need me for this conversation. No one believes me anyway."

The bell over the entrance rang again, signaling their first customer of the day, and Arianne glanced reflexively in that direction, assuming that the newcomer would permanently end discussion of her nonexistent love life. Unfortunately, the person who'd just stepped in was Shane McIntyre. She'd always considered him a buddy, like a third brother, and had enjoyed weekend fishing with him and accompanying him to random events like bowling tournaments and Coach Burton's retirement dinner last spring. But those hadn't been *dates*.

Had they?

Instead of making conversation with any of the Waide men watching, Shane was looking at her as if she were the only one in the room.

Arianne cleared her throat and forced a smile. "Morning, Shane. I was just about to take a coffee break, but I'm sure David would be happy to help you find anything you need."

She resumed her retreat, but didn't get very far.

"Actually, Arianne, I came to talk to you. If you have a minute?"

She stifled a prickle of foreboding. Tanner's erroneous assertion that Shane was interested in her had merely kicked her imagination into overdrive. "Sure, come on back."

Shane followed, waiting until they'd passed into the interior hallway before he said, "Thanks. I didn't really want to have this talk in front of your brothers and dad."

"What talk is that?" With a sidelong glance, Arianne tried to assess the expression on his ruddy face. Shane was handsome in a boyish kind of way, but she'd never been attracted to him.

"Did Tanner happen to mention we ran into each other this morning?"

She nodded, stopping at the recessed alcove where they kept the coffeemaker. "Sugar? Cream?" she asked.

He shook his head. "Just black, thanks. I saw you yesterday, as I was leaving the diner after breakfast. Chatting with Gabriel Sloan."

"Yeah. He wanted to discuss the fall festival."

She reexperienced the triumphant surprise she'd felt when Gabe agreed to help with the fair and the stab of unexpected disappointment when he'd admitted that he'd be leaving Mistletoe soon after. Her instinct had been to protest that leaving was a mistake, but how could she? She'd been the one to question his being here in the first place! If she wanted to make an argument for his staying, she'd have to be patient and bide her time.

She'd ended their conversation by promising to be in touch soon. There'd been a smirk in his voice when he replied, "I don't doubt it."

"The fall festival?" Shane echoed.

Arianne handed him his coffee and poured a second cup. "That's right. Why, what did you think?" She wasn't sure it was a good idea, but she was curious to view the encounter through someone else's eyes. What had Shane seen that would make enough of an impression for him to tattle to her big brother?

"I…I don't know. My sister, Ruthie—you remember her?—she lives in South Carolina now, but back in the day, she was friends with Shay Ortz."

Shay Ortz Templeton.

"Sloan makes me wary," he admitted. "His reputation with women…"

"What reputation?" Arianne asked. "The man barely dates."

He gave her a fond smile that somehow set her teeth on edge. "Just because he's not buying ladies nice dinners doesn't mean he doesn't get around. I heard kitchen tile wasn't all he laid for Nicole Jones. Tara Hunaker hired him to refinish her basement and likes to giggle to anyone who'll listen that the room never did get done, but that Gabriel was worth every penny."

Arianne's stomach lurched. "Tara Hunaker is a floozy reputed to have hit on her husband's attorney in the middle of her divorce proceedings. I'm not putting a lot of stock in what she has to say about Gabe. And I don't see what any of this has to do with me."

Shane shoved his free hand through his hair. "Nothing, really. Except that after I talked to Tanner this morning, I realized that I'd sounded…jealous."

Some of the starch went out of her spine. "So did you come over here to set the record straight?" she asked hopefully. "Make sure Tanner didn't give me the wrong idea?"

"No." Shane swallowed, suddenly making Arianne wish she could add a belt of Irish whiskey to her coffee. "I came because I forced myself to admit I *was* jealous. Irrationally so—I'm not suggesting there's anything between you and Sloan. Even if he's sleeping with all his female clients—"

"Like Quinn?" Arianne asked, her tone ice. "Or Barb Echols?"

"Well, n-no." Shane's complexion flushed dark red as he tried to regroup. "Obviously not them. They're decent women. Like you! You're the one I wanted to talk about, not him. Arianne, I think…I think there could be something special between us."

Arianne had seen "special." She witnessed it firsthand every day. Even after all these years, her parents' faces still lit up when they saw each other across a room. Tanner had given up life in Atlanta and came home to Mistletoe because he'd never been able to forget Lilah Baum. And David had experienced love at first sight when he met Rachel, the wife for whom he would gladly move heaven and earth.

"Shane." She kept her voice gentle, biting her tongue against every bad cliché she'd ever heard. What was she supposed to do, tell him she treasured his friendship? That she loved him like a brother?

When the only words she could think of seemed trite to the point of insulting, she simply shook her head. "I don't feel that way."

He blinked. "But would you be willing to give it a shot? Maybe go on a real date sometime and see—"

"No, thank you. But I'm flattered that you asked." She started to pat his arm then checked herself, not wanting to be condescending. "I should get back to work now."

"Yeah." He didn't meet her eyes. "I don't want to hold you up. Thanks for the coffee."

He fled as if his jeans were on fire.

Damn. She bit the inside of her cheek, but couldn't think how to make this any less awkward for him. Maybe she could let a few days go by to ease the sting, then have lunch with him. Or a movie. A decidedly nonromantic movie with a group of friends.

"Is it safe for us to come back now?" she heard Tanner ask from the doorway. His voice was sympathetic. "We didn't want to interrupt."

"I appreciate that," she said. Her brothers were pains in the butt, but she adored them.

"Everything okay?" David asked.

"Just peachy." She smiled at them, then rejoined her father in the main part of the store. He was busy helping bald Mr. Jebson compare camping equipment.

Business picked up over the next hour, and Arianne was grateful to stay busy. She answered gardening questions for two little old ladies, ordered a new shipment of saws, rang up purchases for four customers and told a woman over the phone that while they didn't officially have gift cards for purchase, Arianne would print some sort of certificate for her husband's birthday and have Zachariah sign it.

Eventually she hit a lull and couldn't help thinking about Shane's unanticipated confession, his optimism that they could build something special. Arianne knew instinctively that she would never reciprocate the sentiment. In fact, one of the reasons she'd always felt so at ease in his company was because he was so…safe. There'd never been any sexual tension.

Arianne was known among family and friends as being cheerfully fearless—which was mostly true—but Waides didn't mess around when it came to love. They fell hard, and Arianne had never been one for half measures. She dated, but with the exception of some high school heartbreaks, she'd guarded her heart.

She hated to think what could happen if she carelessly gave it to the wrong guy.

Chapter Five

Gabe had just started cooking dinner—which, tonight, involved dumping a can of soup into a pot—when his cell phone buzzed and vibrated across the countertop. He saw Waide Supply on the caller ID and considered not answering. What had he been thinking yesterday? He'd been in a strange mood after encountering his father. When he'd seen Arianne, it had been as if something clicked in his brain—help her with the festival, make that his casual farewell after thirty years in this town.

By the time he'd arrived home with his groceries, the idea had begun to seem like more damn trouble than it was worth. There wasn't anyone here to whom he owed a farewell. Still, he'd given his word.

With a sigh, he snatched up the phone. "Gabe Sloan."

"You know, for a guy whose living is dependent on paying customers being able to contact you, you're not that easy to track down," Arianne scolded lightly.

"Yet you managed."

"Ever thought about getting business cards? If you need help creating them—"

"Don't tell me. When you're not managing the store or drafting community volunteers, you design business cards."

"Me? No. But Chloe Malcolm does some great marketing work. She put together our Web site for the store." She paused. "I don't suppose you have a Web site?"

"Miss Waide, as much as I appreciate your helpful advice—"

She guffawed, an unfeminine but admirably unselfconscious sound.

"—now's not really the time for me to be building business. I'm leaving soon," he reminded her, the words warming him. Every time he said it, he felt stronger. Freer.

Arianne was silent a moment. "Do you know where you're going?"

Even if he did, he wouldn't give that information to his would-be stalker. Perhaps that wasn't fair—Arianne had never shown much interest in him before now. After he helped her and Quinn with this festival, she'd go on with her sheltered life and forget all about him.

But just to be on the safe side, he wasn't leaving her a forwarding address.

He redirected the conversation. "I assume you're calling about the fair?"

"A bunch of the volunteers are meeting at Whiteberry tomorrow evening. Six-thirty, in the cafeteria. Think you can join us?"

He had some landscaping work to do for Linda Berdino tomorrow, but it got dark earlier every day. "Sure."

"Great! Then I guess I'll see you there." She drew the sentence out, as if there might be more she wanted to say.

"Good night, Miss Waide," he said firmly. He disconnected and turned his attention to the now-boiling beef-vegetable soup.

The irritating thing about Arianne Waide was not her stubbornness or unsolicited advice, it was her knack for asking really good questions. Where *was* he going? Another small town? Maybe in Tennessee or North Carolina? He'd visited cousins in Birmingham years ago and thought Alabama had its charms.

Deciding to leave was a good first step, but there was a lot he'd need to do. He couldn't just throw a bunch of stuff in a duffel bag and take off in his truck…could he?

No. He'd been able to build a living here as a handyman at first because of his notoriety and later because he was really good at what he did. But if he showed up somewhere new, a tall stranger with no local references, he'd be hard-pressed to make ends meet. And he had to decide what to do with this place.

He carried his bowl to the breakfast bar, looking around him. When the Mitchells had put this semiconverted barn on the market, no one had wanted to invest in finishing the renovations. But Gabe had the skills and resources to complete the most necessary repairs and hadn't cared enough to be bothered by the superficial ones. He wasn't sure whether anyone would be interested in buying, but he knew he'd at least be selling it in better condition than he'd purchased it.

A rental property, maybe? Assuming he could find someone, rent would provide some monthly income while he got on his feet elsewhere, but he disliked the idea. He was finally contemplating liberation from Mistletoe, and owning a rental home here would be one remaining tether he didn't need.

What about Jeremy? It was telling that when Gabe considered his last ties to town, he thought of an old barn before his own father.

Then again, that tie had been severed years ago. Gabe had been scared and guilt-stricken, but his father hadn't noticed. All he'd seen through his contempt was someone who'd dishonored "the sanctity of marriage." Gabe had thought, rather hysterically, that his father was more upset about Gabe's involvement with a married woman than the fact *two people were dead.*

"You're a minor, and I'm legally bound to house you," Jeremy Sloan had said. "But as soon as you're of age, get the hell out."

Congratulations, Pops. You'll be getting your wish soon.

ARIANNE PULLED UP to the school at about the same time as her sister-in-law, Rachel. Both of them parked in the bus lanes that were empty for the evening. Arianne got out of her car, then bent to pick up the bags of food and drink tray. A few feet away, she watched as Rachel gathered Bailey's diaper bag and unfastened the baby's car seat.

"I feel like I should offer you assistance," Arianne called, "but…"

Rachel laughed. "I appreciate the thought. Here, let me get the door for you." With the diaper bag on her shoulder and her daughter sleeping across her chest in some kind of odd sling, Rachel actually had both hands free.

Arianne grinned. "You look like you're mastering this Mommy gig."

"Some days more than others," Rachel admitted.

They filed into the cafeteria, where Quinn and Lilah were seated at a long table. With the festival meeting tonight, they'd decided simply to stay late after school, working on lesson plans and replacing outdated art projects and essays on the classroom walls. Arianne had volunteered to bring dinner so that the four of them could eat and catch up before everyone else arrived.

While Quinn came to Arianne's side to help carry the food, Lilah made a beeline for Rachel, peering into the durable cloth infant carrier with such delighted awe that Arianne wondered how long it would be before she was made an aunt twice over.

"That smells so good," Rachel said on a near moan. "When I was pregnant, everyone teased me about eating for two, but my appetite's actually increased since she was born. Now that I'm nursing, I feel like I'm starving all the time."

"Well, you look great," Quinn said, handing her the iced tea that was marked decaf. "Women who've given birth recently shouldn't be that fit. It's not fair to the rest of us mere mortals."

Lilah laughed. "Says one of the most gorgeous women in the county."

Quinn looked especially nice tonight in a cute wraparound dress and high ponytail that was both stylish and playful.

"Thank you," Arianne told Lilah. "Now maybe she'll believe me when I tell her Patrick can't help but notice her."

"Ari!" Quinn darted a glance toward the hallway, as if making sure no one was around to overhear. "It's not like I don't have the confidence to talk to a guy. It's just more…complicated when he works with you. Huge potential for awkwardness."

Arianne thought of the uncomfortable conversation she'd had yesterday morning with Shane McIntyre. "You may have a point. I got ambushed yesterday by an admission I wasn't expecting and awkward barely begins to cover it."

"Who?" Quinn asked.

"Shane?" Lilah asked, her voice sympathetic. "Tanner mentioned that he came by the store to talk to you. And that he was acting weird at the gas station, freaked out because there might be something between you and Gabe Sloan."

Rachel let out a low whistle. "Gabe Sloan? Talk about the most gorgeous person in the county."

"Arianne got him to agree to help us," Quinn said proudly. "I have to admit, I was surprised, but she did it."

Arianne bit into another fry. Little did her friend know that Gabe's assistance had less to do with her persuasive prowess than his wanting closure with the town.

Oh, *he* probably didn't think of it that way, but Arianne could read between the lines. She hadn't shared with anyone what he'd told her about planning to leave.

"So what happened with Shane?" Quinn asked. "You guys have known each other forever."

"And he's never seemed interested in me romantically, which is why yesterday caught me so off guard. He said he thought we could have something special if I would give it a chance."

Rachel winced. "But you don't see him that way?"

"'Fraid not. I mean, he's a great guy. I'm just more attracted to—" She broke off as the image of Gabe's unsmiling but striking face filled her mind. *Be reasonable, Ari.* Regardless of how physically attractive Gabe was, no woman with common sense would consider a relationship with him. As far as his personal life went, he had issues with a capital *I* and as far as Mistletoe went, he had one foot out the door.

"Shane's just not my type," she concluded lamely. "I told him that I didn't feel the same way."

"You didn't say you still wanted to be friends?" Quinn asked hesitantly.

"No! Although I do hope that."

"And you really didn't have any inkling?" Rachel asked, shifting the baby gently. "Because I can't say I'm all that surprised he likes you. You guys do spend a lot of time together."

"Yeah, but it's always been so platonic." At least on her part. Had she deliberately overlooked something she hadn't wanted to see? Feeling unobservant and perhaps a bit foolish, she changed the subject. "Who has Dele duty tonight?"

Sixty-year-old music teacher Adele Momsen signed up for every volunteer opportunity in town, bursting at the seams with Big Ideas she was eager to share. When she got married eight years ago, she'd wanted her and her groom to lift off from the circular drive of Mistletoe Methodist in a hot-air balloon. The town fathers had quickly vetoed that idea, citing FAA regulations. Her enthusiastic suggestions often ranged from the bizarre to the beyond-budget to the outright someone-could-get-killed. Lilah and Quinn liked to make sure that a specific person diplomatically reined her in before someone else hurt her feelings with more tactless objections.

Lilah raised her index finger, taking on the responsibility for tonight. "I love Dele. She might not be living in the same reality as the rest of us, but her heart's in the right place. Can't say the same about Cici Hunaker."

Cici was known for being something of a control freak; her kids had moved on to middle school and high school, yet she continued to call the chairpersons on Whiteberry's PTA committees to find out if they were still doing things her way. And, if not, to insinuate they were idiots.

"Hey, speaking of the Hunakers," Arianne began.

"Yes?" Rachel prompted.

Mentally kicking herself, Arianne shoved a couple more fries into her mouth. Had she really been about to ask if any of them had heard rumors about Gabe Sloan and Tara Hunaker? Even if what Shane had implied *was* true, Gabe and Tara were consenting adults. Why did the thought of them together bother Arianne so much?

Because I'd like to think he has more discerning taste than that. Not *because I'm jealous.*

The baby chose that moment to wake up crying, and Lilah offered to unlock her classroom and let Rachel nurse Bailey in private. As the two women excused themselves from the cafeteria, Quinn and Arianne cleaned up the trash from dinner.

"I'm glad you'll be meeting Patrick tonight," Quinn admitted. "I'm interested in getting your opinion of him."

"And you know I'll be happy to give one," Arianne joked. But a foreign sentiment was squirming around inside her. Uncertainty.

She was known for reading people well and giving smart advice, but now she questioned that reputation. After all, she'd entirely missed any sign that one of her close friends was falling for her and, over the past week, she'd found herself thinking too often of Gabriel Sloan. There wasn't anything strange about noticing he was hot or wanting better for him than the informal exile the town had sentenced him to years ago. But she'd fallen asleep more than once imagining what it would be like to kiss him and had stalled last night getting off the phone with him simply because she liked listening to his voice.

She might be too wise to lose her heart to a man like Gabe, but if she admitted to her friends that she was starting to enjoy his gruff, growly voice, they might worry that she was losing her mind.

PATRICK FLANNERY TURNED OUT to be every bit as attractive as Lilah and Quinn had said—just under six feet with smiling, bright blue eyes and rich brown hair. But his most appealing quality, in Arianne's opinion, was the way he kept glancing toward Quinn. Especially when he didn't think anyone was watching. When Quinn caught him, her pretty face flushed pink, and Arianne grinned, mentally betting herself that she'd be fitted for another bridesmaid dress within the year.

Still, for all that Patrick was a nice-looking man, he was rendered nearly invisible the second Gabe Sloan set foot into the cafeteria. A sudden pulse of hyperawareness left Arianne as unsteady as if the room had rocked beneath her feet. He was ruggedly sensual in a brown leather jacket and worn jeans; his hair was slightly damp as if he'd grabbed a quick shower before coming to the meeting.

Gabe Sloan, in the shower. A hot shiver went through her. *Steady, girl.*

"Gabe!" Hoping that none of her baser instincts were visible in her expression, she beamed at him, quickly crossing toward him.

As Arianne threaded between the narrow cafeteria tables and the scattering of women already seated, that earlier uncertainty she'd been feeling reared its ugly head, and she second-guessed herself. She'd wanted Gabe to feel more included in Mistletoe, but aside from Patrick, he was the only man present. He stood out dramatically in this small assembly of women, against the surreal backdrop of a playground mural in bright primary colors and low-to-the-ground bench seating meant to accommodate even the smallest kindergartener.

Had she made a mistake asking him to come here? She banished the thought almost immediately. Change was difficult, but that didn't make stagnation or withdrawal healthier options.

When she stopped in front of him, Gabe dipped his head in acknowledgment. "Miss Waide."

It should've sounded silly—she was Arianne or Ari to everyone she knew—but something about the way it came out in Gabe's low voice conjured the Western frontier and mysterious gunslingers who were good with their hands.

"Call me Arianne. Please."

"All right."

She swallowed, breaking eye contact. "Come on, there's someone you should meet." Arianne knew everyone's eyes were on her and Gabe as they approached Patrick, who sat at a table with Lilah, Quinn and Dele Momsen. Rachel had yet to return from feeding the baby.

"Gabe, this is Patrick Flannery, Mistletoe Elementary's newest teacher and our town's newest resident. I'm sure you'll make him feel welcome," she babbled.

Gabe quirked an eyebrow at her as if challenging her assertion, but he was perfectly cordial as he shook hands with Patrick. "Gabe Sloan, nice to meet you."

Dele scooted over on the bench so that Gabe could sit between her and Patrick.

"Pleased to make your acquaintance," Patrick said,

glancing around with a self-conscious smile. "Don't get me wrong—there are worse fates than being surrounded by women—but I'm glad not to be the only guy. So, you're from Mistletoe? Most everyone I've met seems to have grown up here."

"My whole life," Gabe said.

Arianne wondered if anyone else heard the bitter undertone of his voice. Her attention was wrenched away from Gabe when she saw Kasey Kerrigan, juggling a large box of printed flyers, as well as art supplies they were going to use to make eye-catching posters. Leaving the two men to chat, Arianne went to Kasey's side.

"Thanks," Kasey said as she handed over a plastic bag and some neon poster board.

"No problem," Arianne said. She smiled at the older woman, but then stiffened as she saw who was entering the cafeteria behind them.

The Hunaker sisters.

Too bad flasks would be considered inappropriate at a PTA-related meeting because Arianne thought that a little hard liquor might take the edge off dealing with Tara and Cici. Both women were in their forties, well preserved through expensive cosmetics and a few surgical weekend trips to Atlanta. They had matching smiles that made Arianne think of great white sharks with collagen injections. Neither Hunaker sister actually had a child currently enrolled in Whiteberry, but since the same could be said of several volunteers—Ari and Gabe included—that didn't give the committee license to boot the siblings.

Arianne increased her stride, hoping not to get sucked into small talk with Cici and Tara, but even with the additional distance, she caught Gabe's name, followed by a flurry of hectic whispering.

Kasey and Arianne sat on the empty bench across from the men and were joined by Rachel and her now-content daughter. Then Quinn stood to welcome everyone and make it clear how much the school appreciated their support.

"The fall festival is a long-standing tradition, and I know that with your help, we can make this year's the best yet! Now I'm going to turn things over to my co-chair Lilah Waide…."

Lilah outlined the subcommittees and specific positions that needed to be filled. When she mentioned the cakewalk and annual bake-off, though, a hand shot up from Arianne's table.

"Not to be a bother, but could I interrupt for just a sec?" Dele asked sweetly. "I revere our town traditions—I've lived in Mistletoe more than fifty years—but there's no reason we can't improve on them, right? Reach for new heights?"

Lilah's smile flickered nervously, but she nodded. "Change can keep things fresh."

"What if instead of a whole bunch of people individually baking cakes, we banded together? I saw this news piece on a middle school attempting to make the world's largest cupcake and there was mention of a Canadian slab of fudge that was over two tons. Wouldn't it be neat if Mistletoe could set one of those records for the biggest cake?"

Two tons of fudge? Just how much cake was Dele proposing? The silence in the cafeteria got very loud, emphasized by a single derisive titter in the back. One of the Hunakers, no doubt.

"Well," Lilah began. "That certainly is an *ambitious* idea! But I doubt we could get all the logistics squared away in only two weeks. Would you mind if I write this in our notes as something to discuss for future years?"

Dele beamed. "I think that'd be just fine, Lilah. Thank you."

It wasn't until Quinn began differentiating between the booths that they hoped would break even financially, those there for fun despite not being moneymakers, versus the ones they actually expected to profit on that Dele's hand shot back up again.

"I had a fundraiser idea," Dele said proudly. "A couple of years ago, during the July Fourth celebration, officials like the mayor and principal agreed to sit in a dunk tank. Citizens lined up to pay for a chance to soak them!"

Lilah and Quinn exchanged glances. As Dele's ideas went, this one was completely sane.

"Sounds terrific," Lilah said, "with the possible exception of the weather. I'm not sure it would be warm enough—"

"Oh, I don't think we should dunk them!" Dele interjected. "I think we should make them walk the plank. As part of our costume competition, we already have a best pirate category, so it just makes sense! Think about our students in their best buccaneer garb, paying for a

chance to march their favorite—or least favorite—
teachers off a plank at swordpoint."

"I'm sorry, did you say off a plank?" Cici Hunaker
echoed incredulously.

Dele spun around, nodding eagerly over her shoulder.
"Sounds like fun, dontcha think?"

"And this would be the plank of the handy pirate
ship we just happen to have sitting in town square?"
Cici rejoined.

Tara snickered, and Dele's face fell. Looking at the
older woman's crushed expression, Arianne's loathing
of the Hunakers soared to new heights.

Even Quinn was openly glaring at the two women.
"I should remind everyone that we're all working
toward the same goal and the first rule of brainstorm-
ing is that you don't criticize ideas as they're flowing."

"Even the ridiculous ones?" Tara muttered.

"Actually—" Gabe turned in his seat, ostensibly ad-
dressing Dele, although his voice carried throughout
the room "—I like your idea, Mrs. Momsen."

"You do?"

He reached out to awkwardly pat the woman's
hunched shoulder. "Absolutely. There are plenty of people in this town I wouldn't mind sending off the plank."

Across the table from him, Arianne was dimly aware
of muffled laughs and even one or two gasps, but none
of those reactions truly registered with her. She was
fixated on Gabe's profile as he exchanged hesitant
smiles with Dele.

Heaven help me, he has dimples.

Chapter Six

Quinn and Lilah called the meeting to a close just in time—over the past hour and a half, the cheerfully decorated cafeteria walls had started closing in on Gabe. *I need to get out of here.* He was preoccupied enough with his growing unease that he nodded at something Patrick said without really hearing it.

"Great!" The other man clapped him congenially on the shoulder. "You just let me know what night works best for you."

Gabe paused, not sure what he'd just agreed to, but telling himself that, whatever it was, it couldn't be any stranger than telling Adele Momsen he'd build her a pirate ship. Rather, a partial facade of a ship. Kasey, from the family-owned Kerrigan Farms, had said there was a company that rented "bouncies" and ball pits—popular attractions for kids who wanted to jump inside inflatable structures or play amidst hundreds of spongy balls. She thought she remembered something from their catalog where participants could literally dive into an open pit. Assuming her phone call to them tomorrow was productive, Gabe would start work on a raised platform that would emulate the deck of a ship, complete with a plank.

By Gabe's early teens, he'd been antsy, wanting to leave Mistletoe and the proximity of an unloving father who made him feel vaguely guilty for his very existence. Looking ahead to the financial independence he'd need to escape, Gabe had started mowing lawns and helping elderly neighbors—including Adele Momsen's mother—clean out their rain gutters. He'd kept an organized spiral notebook of his clients and what they'd paid him. To this day, he kept an organized to-do list and studied it each morning over coffee.

A couple of weeks ago, it had been a simple, even predictable, compilation: pick up materials at Waide Supply, meet with Linda Berdino about her yard, tell the Winchesters that they really did need to hire a certified plumber.

And then Arianne Waide had happened.

Gabe's list had morphed radically. *One, find new home. Two, build pirate ship.*

Patrick Flannery shrugged into his jacket. "So I'll catch you later for that pool game."

Three, make new friend. Apparently. "Sure," Gabe said. At least now he knew what he'd agreed to.

With a nod and parting smile for Mrs. Momsen, he made a beeline for the exit and the promise of fresh air. He was almost there when Tara Hunaker sidled into his peripheral vision.

"Gabriel?" Her low, smoky voice might have been

more seductive if it weren't so affected. And if he didn't know her better.

The week he'd spent working for her had ensured that he would never look at her and see a beautiful woman.

"I wanted to apologize for my knee-jerk reaction to the pirate fundraiser," she said, her expression beseeching.

"Good idea," he said. "Mrs. Momsen's right over there."

"Fair enough. I'll talk to her as soon as we're done. Have to say, I never would have expected to see you here, but I'm glad—"

"Gabe!"

Arianne bounded toward them with all the restraint and self-consciousness of a puppy, a complete contrast to Tara's studied expressions and come-hither voice.

Despite whatever chaos Arianne had wreaked on his life, he'd choose dealing with her over Tara Hunaker any day. He flicked the latter a dismissive glance. "If you'll excuse us?"

He stepped to the side and waited for Arianne to reach him.

At close range, her smile was nearly blinding. "You were *magnificent!*" She threw her arms around him.

Gabe stiffened. She was *hugging* him? People didn't hug him. He wasn't... He didn't— "Miss Waide?" *Unhand me.*

Not that her embrace was unpleasant. Quite the contrary. She was soft and lush, round in exactly the right places despite her diminutive size. Her warmth radiated through him, the scent of raspberries teasing his senses.

He was startled by the urge to pull her tight and breathe her in.

His newfound claustrophobia kicked in with a vengeance, and he jerked back a step. He half expected her to look stung by the rudeness, but instead, her rueful smile was apologetic.

"That was probably overkill, hmm?" she admitted. "I do tend to come on strong."

"I hadn't noticed," he deadpanned.

"I just wanted to say thank you before you disappeared into the night. You made sweet Mrs. Momsen's entire year, agreeing to help with that ship."

He shifted his weight, unused to this level of gratitude. When he fenced in someone's backyard, they usually just handed him a check. "Hey, she's the one who had the good idea. I'm just the hired muscle."

"Except that we're not paying you," Arianne reminded him with a laugh. "Oh, but we'll definitely reimburse you for the supplies. Jennifer Gideon is the PTA treasurer—just make sure she gets your receipts. And we'll help with construction, too. It's too much work for one person in such a short time frame. Patrick and I—"

"You have a lot of experience with carpentry?" Gabe interrupted.

"I helped my brothers build a tree house! Although, technically, it collapsed," she added, not looking the least bit abashed by this admission.

He raised an eyebrow.

"It was an educational experience! Now that I've learned from my mistakes, I—"

"Night," Patrick called as he walked past toward the exit. "It was nice to meet you, Arianne."

"You, too." She shot the man one of her uninhibited, all-encompassing grins, and something sharp shifted inside Gabe.

Something like…possessiveness? Though he'd told himself he didn't want to be saddled with an unrelentingly cheerful sidekick, he was growing accustomed to—maybe even appreciative of—those smiles.

"And I'll see you this week for that pool game?" Patrick asked. But he didn't give Gabe a chance to answer before he quickly shifted his gaze back to Arianne. "Hey! Why don't you join us? You and Quinn? That is, if you think she'd—"

"Oh, she would!" Arianne assured him, her tone delighted. "It's a date. So to speak."

Gabe simply stared, his strange new to-do list slipping further out of his control. *Four, go on double date.*

QUINN SHIFTED in the passenger seat—she'd been uncharacteristically fidgety in the ten minutes since they'd left her house. "So would you classify this as a date, or—?"

"If it's not, you certainly went through a lot of trouble with your appearance for no reason," Arianne teased. "I lost count of the times you've asked how you look."

Quinn sniffed. "Only twice! But I see your point. I'm being ridiculous, aren't I? It's not like I never date."

"True, but when was the last time you went out with a guy you were really interested in? If it helps your nerves at all," Arianne offered, "I think he likes you, too.

I got the impression Patrick only asked me to come play pool because he was using me as a way to invite you."

"Well, I appreciate you sacrificing your Thursday night for my sake," Quinn said.

Arianne sent her a sidelong grin. "Hey, there are worse ways to spend an evening than shooting pool with friends." *And Gabe.*

What were his thoughts on tonight's outing? When Patrick had asked her about making this a foursome, she'd seized the chance to help Quinn jump-start her love life, not pausing to check with Gabe first. Arianne hadn't spoken directly to him since Tuesday night's volunteer meeting, although she had left a message on his cell phone that Kasey Kerrigan had put a deposit on the ball pit and that the principal had approved their walk-the-plank benefit.

She turned the car into the parking lot of the pool-hall-slash-dance-hall. On Tap was a favorite local hangout, known for its outdated jukebox and eye-watering hot wings. To kick off the weekend, the owners offered half-price pool and various drink specials on Thursdays, so Arianne wasn't surprised to find that the lot was nearly three-quarters full.

"You're sure you aren't the tiniest bit anxious?" Quinn asked as Arianne parked the car.

"Me? Why would I be?"

Quinn rolled her eyes. "Gabe Sloan? Maybe you remember him? Guy you asked out who said no, and yet here you are on a—"

"It's definitely not a date for us. We're more like…the

chaperones for you and Patrick. But don't worry. I promise to turn a blind eye if you two crazy kids want to make out."

They got out of the car, and Arianne spotted Gabe's red truck among the other vehicles. A frisson of anticipation zinged through her—involuntary and completely unwise. Still, she heard herself ask, "Just for the sake of argument, if I wanted to know how *I* looked—"

Quinn flashed a thumbs-up. "Gorgeous. Different but gorgeous."

"Thanks. I think."

Though both women were wearing dark jeans, Arianne's top was nothing like her friend's fuzzy pastel sweater. Arianne had second-guessed her first choice— a long-sleeved V-neck—because of how revealing it would be when she leaned across the pool table. She didn't need to distract her opponents with cleavage to win. Instead, she'd gone with a black turtleneck that looked fairly dramatic with her coloring. She'd braided her hair and selected a pair of long silver earrings Rachel had given her for Christmas one year.

The noise hit them before they'd even reached the front door—a buzz of voices, billiard balls clicking against each other as they spun across the green and the guitar-heavy angst of an '80s hair-band ballad. Inside, Arianne felt absorbed by the sound and energy of the crowd.

"There they are," Quinn said from behind her.

The men had already secured a pool table and were selecting cues. Gabe took a practice shot, and Arianne's mouth went dry as she watched the play of muscles beneath his T-shirt. The scuffed leather jacket he'd worn the other night was draped over a nearby chair.

Quinn laughed suddenly. "I feel like I missed the uniform memo."

"What?" With disciplined effort, Arianne did not check out Gabe's denim-clad backside as he bent again.

"You two look like twins. Or at least partners in crime," she amended.

Gabe and Arianne were both clad in monochromatic black. Patrick was more colorful in a red-and-blue-striped shirt with khakis. He brightened visibly when he spotted the women approaching.

"Quinn! Ari. Looks like we just beat the rush," Patrick observed. "This was the last table available."

Gabe nodded his hello. "Ladies." His gaze flicked from Quinn to Arianne. His features were unreadable, but Arianne could have sworn that his glance lingered. Her skin warmed. Did he like what he saw?

"Can I get either of you a drink?" Patrick volunteered.

"I'll take a beer." Arianne pulled a five-dollar bill out of her pocket.

"I'll come with you," Quinn said.

Patrick grinned at her, then turned to Gabe. "Ready for a refill?"

"Nah, I'm good." He'd placed the triangle on the felt and was racking the balls.

The two teachers headed for the bar, leaving Arianne and Gabe alone.

"I hope this is okay with you," she said. "Quinn and I joining your boys' night?"

He raised his eyes just long enough to give her a pointed look. Was he implying that it was unlike her to worry about boundaries?

She cleared her throat. "You got my message about the plank and ball pit? We're officially a 'go.'"

"Yep."

"Have you had time to think about the actual ship yet?"

"Yep."

She walked toward the wall where the cues hung. "So, are you any good at pool?" If he said yep, she was bashing him with one of the sticks.

"Not bad." But there was a spark of underlying mischief in his tone that made her suspect he was being modest. "You?"

"I hold my own." She studied a stick, then rolled it over the table to make sure it wasn't warped. "My brothers taught me to play. Tanner used to be the black sheep of our family. For a while, I thought he might skip college and just hustle pool for a living. But he went on to get a prestigious degree and a job in finance. Just goes to show people can change, huh?"

Gabe leaned against the side of the table, his expression pained. "If that's your way of suggesting I—"

"I wasn't 'suggesting' anything, only making conversation." She peered up at him with innocent eyes. "Do you always think everything's about you?"

He shook his head at her denial. "Like I'm going to trust someone dressed as a junior cat burglar?"

"You're one to talk," she rejoined, raking her gaze over him. "Quinn said we look like twins."

That startled a rusty laugh out of him. "Arianne, we couldn't be less alike if we tried."

After Patrick and Quinn returned with the beverages, it soon became clear that Gabe and Arianne had at least one thing in common—they were definitely better at pool than their companions.

Quinn reached blindly toward the wall rack and grabbed the closest cue stick to her. "Do we have to play by the formal rules of calling a shot for it to count?" She wrinkled her nose. "If I have to give up the ones I make out of sheer dumb luck, I could be in trouble."

"How about for the first game, while we're getting warmed up, we only call the last pocket to win?" Patrick suggested. He grinned boyishly. "I'm out of practice, but even when I played, I was never exactly pool-shark material. No pointing and laughing, I beg you."

"And," Quinn added, "no *accidentally* knocking your opponents' balls in just to give yourself competition."

Arianne studied the ceiling. "I don't know what you're talking about."

"I'm starting to think," Patrick said, "that Quinn and I should not be on the same team. No offense, Quinn."

"None taken," she agreed cheerfully. "It would be a slaughter."

"So how do we want to pair up?" Arianne asked. "Girls against guys?"

"Or you and Patrick can take on Quinn and me," Gabe suggested.

That met with everyone's approval, and they flipped a coin to see which team would break. Patrick did an all right job with that task, although no balls were pocketed. Quinn put in a stripe but scratched in the process. Arianne knocked in two solids before misjudging a bank, and then it was Gabe's turn. He sank three consecutive balls, one of which was a beautiful behind-the-back shot.

"All right, now you're just showing off," Arianne chided.

He dazzled her with a lazy smile. "Maybe."

It was *criminal* that he had a smile like that and so seldom used it.

On the other hand, at least he wasn't abusing its power—irresponsibly flashing it at unsuspecting women. When he grinned at her, Arianne couldn't even look away. She wanted to go to him, run her thumb over the dimpled brackets along his mouth, brush her finger over those lips…

"Um, guys?" Quinn's voice was hesitant. "It's still our team's turn, right?"

Embarrassment warmed Arianne as she realized she'd lost track of time and place staring at Gabe. Then again, he'd been staring back. His smile had disappeared, but he looked no less sexy without it. *Stop gawking already!* Arianne whirled around to the railing where her beer sat. She sipped slowly, taking a moment to compose herself. With her back turned, she missed Gabe's shot.

Apparently so did he. She caught his soft "damn" and smiled against her glass. Her flustered reaction to him wouldn't be nearly as humiliating if he was equally rattled.

They completed another round of turns with Patrick making the only shot. Though Quinn missed, she made strategic progress by leaving absolutely nothing for Arianne. Gabe lined up a shot, but put too much spin on the ball, ricocheting it off the corner tip instead of into the pocket.

He ran a hand through his hair. "Patrick, you're up. I believe it's my turn to get drinks? Anyone need anything?"

When Quinn and Patrick both accepted a second round, Arianne slid off the stool where she'd been perched. "I'll help carry."

Of course you will, Gabe thought ruefully. Last week he'd had the exasperated thought that Arianne Waide was difficult to escape. She had a certain aura of inevitability, but he no longer found that annoying. When had that changed?

Maybe at Tuesday's festival meeting, when she'd been so protective of grandmotherly Mrs. Momsen and so sincere in her gratitude. In small doses, Arianne's exuberance could be refreshing.

Or maybe his feelings toward her had softened tonight when he'd caught sight of her in the formfitting turtleneck. It was difficult to think of her as nothing more than an adorable pain in the butt when she looked so artlessly sophisticated.

And he wasn't the only one who noticed. As they walked through the crowd, Gabe wondered if she was aware of the way men's gazes followed her. It occurred to him for the first time to be surprised that she, unlike her happily married brothers, was single.

They reached the bar, politely elbowing their way into the waiting throng.

"Lot more crowded tonight than on Wednesdays," Gabe noted.

She slanted an assessing look at him, searching for something.

"What?"

"I have a question that's none of my business."

"And you're showing restraint and decided not to ask?"

"Hell, no. I was just debating the best way to broach it." She smiled at him unrepentantly.

Gabe smothered a laugh, not wanting to encourage her. "You're something else."

"Lovable," she supplied promptly. "That's what my family calls me."

"Maybe when you're in earshot."

"Why, Mr. Sloan, did you just make a joke?"

"No, I was serious." But he grinned down at her.

"So why don't we see more of you in here on the weekends?" she asked. "You used to drop by on occasional Fridays and Saturdays."

"My God, you really *are* a stalker."

The blush climbing her cheeks belied the dismissive way she rolled her eyes. "Don't be ridiculous. It's not like I memorized your schedule. It's just that you don't exactly blend into the crowd."

His humor faded. She didn't know how accurate the statement was. Even before his escalating flirtation and doomed one-night stand with Shay had made him an outcast in Mistletoe, he'd never even felt as though he belonged in his own home. He had early memories of feeling self-conscious in school when the class worked on crafting homemade gifts for Mother's Day and events where parents were invited to participate.

"I meant because you're tall," Arianne said, the soft apology in her voice like a blade.

He flinched away from her pity. "Well, we can't all be short."

"What can I get—" The bartender, who had just handed over two drinks to the people in front of them, began the question by rote but stopped when he saw it was Gabe. "Usual?"

"No, make it a beer tonight," Gabe said. "Four beers."

The man did a double take. "Really?"

Gabe glared.

"Coming right up."

Would Arianne attribute the man's surprise to Gabe's actually being here with others?

"I normally stick to sodas," he found himself explaining.

"You don't drink?"

"I just ordered a beer, didn't I?" How could someone like Arianne Waide, with her cheerful can-do attitude and supportive family and friends, understand why Gabe felt like he couldn't indulge in the luxury of relaxing, of just letting go? In the past year especially, he'd felt compelled to stay on his guard. It wasn't that he was afraid of fueling gossip. It was more... Anger, he realized.

Tara Hunaker hiring him as a flimsy ploy to seduce

him, Mike Renault—the closest thing Gabe had to a friend—moving to Athens over the summer, Gabe's own certainty that his father was never going to forgive him for sins real or imagined. If he wasn't guarded with his emotions, they might spill over in dark ways. *I should've left a long time ago.*

The bartender passed over their beers, and Gabe handed Arianne hers. "Cheers."

Back at the pool table they found Patrick and Quinn deep in conversation. By their body language, it was easy to see that the attraction between them was mutual, and Gabe wasn't the least surprised when Patrick sheepishly asked if Arianne and Gabe would mind playing the next game alone.

"Somehow Quinn tricked me into agreeing to dance." He smiled into the woman's eyes. "Don't say I didn't warn you—I'm actually better at pool than dancing."

She laughed. "I'm good enough on the dance floor to compensate."

"Lead on," he said, looking as if he'd follow her into traffic if that's what she wanted.

Arianne watched them go, and Gabe noticed the wistful tinge to her expression. Again he wondered why she was single.

Gabe could think of a dozen guys easy who would be happy to date her. The thought set his teeth on edge, and he grabbed the triangle. "You know how to play nine ball?"

"Of course."

"Best out of three?"

She held out her hand. "I'll rack."

He passed over the triangle, and their fingers brushed. There was no reason, except for prolonged celibacy, for his blood to beat harder in his veins. After all, it was a mere touch, not the full-body contact of her hug the other night. Still, as he watched her set the balls in the appropriate diamond, he couldn't quite marshal his physical reaction or the direction of his thoughts. Arianne was a beautiful woman with a very sexy body.

And a hell of a pool player, he was forced to admit when she beat him handily in the first round with a four-nine combination.

He raised his beer in salute. "Impressive."

She grinned over her shoulder, reaching for her own drink. "Hey, I have moves."

"I'll bet." He'd said that *aloud?* He busied himself setting up the next game to avoid her reaction.

She broke. After he'd bent to take his turn, she said, "You know when I said earlier that I'd seen you in here on the weekends? Your height wasn't the only reason I noticed you."

His shot went wild. Was she flirting with him? The prospect was far more tempting than it should have been.

"No comments from the peanut gallery while I'm shooting," he admonished.

"All right." She stepped forward and called the one in the side left pocket. Then she stalled under the pretext of aiming. "You're a memorable guy, Gabe."

"I'm aware," he grated. First thing tomorrow, he was

calling his cousins, calling Mike Renault, calling any damn person who might be able to help him make an anonymous fresh start somewhere.

"You turned down Candy Beemis," she said, sounding awestruck.

"If you say so. Take your freaking shot already."

She missed and moved aside, seeming unfazed. "I was buying a drink and heard her ask you to dance. You told her no. That was extremely memorable and possibly the only refusal she's ever received. Candy's the most attractive woman in Mistletoe."

Gabe lined up his shot and told himself to keep his eye on the ball. Instead, he lifted his head, holding Arianne's gaze. "She's not even close."

Arianne sucked in a breath and went silent. *Thank God.* He knocked in the first five balls. She sank the six, but just barely. He knew even as she called the seven-nine combo that she wouldn't make it.

He won the game.

"Guess I deserved that," she muttered. "I let—"

"Arianne?"

They both turned at the masculine voice. Shane McIntyre was approaching—slightly unsteady on his feet—his round face a scrolling billboard of emotions. Surprise, hurt, indignation. More hurt.

"Shane."

Gabe recognized the note of pity in Arianne's voice. He'd heard it directed at him earlier in the evening and could just imagine how it abraded the other man's nerves. Had she dumped the guy? Gabe didn't remember hearing their names linked together, but then, he wasn't exactly in the loop.

The man curled his lip. "I don't believe this," he said, his words faintly slurred. "What are you doing with *him?*"

Arianne narrowed her eyes, all traces of sympathy erased. "I assume that question was rhetorical because we both know I don't owe you any explanations for how I spend my time."

"Right." He gave a vicious nod and took a step forward. "Because I'm no one important, just someone who *cares* about you."

Gabe laid a hand on the guy's shoulder, determined that he wasn't getting a single inch closer to Ari in his current state. "McIntyre, maybe you should save this discussion for later and just let the lady enjoy her evening."

Shane rounded on him. "Let her enjoy *you,* you mean? You're not worthy of taking her trash out, you son of a—" He broke off, eyes wide, at the sight of Gabe's arm drawn back.

Gabe, who hadn't even realized he'd made a fist, was far more horrified than his would-be target. Poleaxed, he dropped his hand to his side. He glanced toward Arianne, wondering if she was appalled by his behavior, and noticed that the pool players at the neighboring tables had paused in their games. Some had drinks in their hands and were surreptitiously watching over the rims while others stared openly. What did they see? A longtime troublemaker agitating one of their own?

As if Shane had sensed a change in energy, he

squared his shoulders in challenge. "What's it going to be, Sloan? Should we take this outside?"

"Of course not!" Arianne interjected. "What is this, junior high?"

At her contemptuous tone, Shane lost his smirk. "Sorry, Arianne. But—

She stepped between the two men. "We're *friends*. And as a friend, I'm telling you to find Nick or Josh to drive you home."

"And leave you with—"

"Now," she said. "Before you do anything else you'll regret tomorrow."

Shane glared at both of them, but wisely shut up. The moment he melted back into the crowd, Arianne exhaled in relief.

"I'll be back in a sec," she told Gabe, betraying no hint of how she felt about his interference. "I want to make sure he asks someone for a lift."

People were no longer staring, but the buzz of their speculative conversations scratched at Gabe's skin. He downed the rest of his beer, wishing he were anywhere else in the world right now. As he set down the empty bottle, he saw Quinn and Patrick returning, their faces flushed with happiness and exertion. He felt like a miscast actor in someone else's movie. He didn't belong in this quaint foursome scene. He was more comfortable in his perennial role as outsider. Arianne should be here with Quinn, Patrick and someone like McIntyre. Well, not McIntyre—he'd behaved like a jackass tonight. Arianne deserved better. *Than either of us.*

He attempted a smile at Quinn, but doubted it was convincing. "Hey, you guys, do me a favor? Tell Arianne that I'm gonna get going. But I'll see everyone Saturday." They were supposed to start initial festival setup downtown.

"But…" Quinn bit her lip. "Sure. Okay."

Gabe nodded to Patrick. "Thanks for inviting me, man."

Despite how the evening had turned out, Patrick had been the first person in a long time to extend a simple, no-strings-attached gesture of friendship. Gabe didn't count Arianne's asking him to dinner. She was anything but simple.

As he passed the bar, he heard her call him but continued his measured strides toward the door, hoping she would assume the noise drowned her out and just let him go. *Good luck with that plan.* He may not have known Arianne long, but he knew her better than that.

She must have rushed, elbowing her way through the boisterous mass of people, to catch up with him just as he stepped out onto the sidewalk.

"You're leaving," she said, full of accusation. "Haven't we already discussed the futility of trying to run away?"

He looked her in the eye, then wished he hadn't. Her fierce expression made him feel like a coward. "I'm not running anywhere. I came, I shot pool, I finished my drink. I'm going home." *Home.* The word burned like acid on his tongue.

She reached up and cupped his cheek. That contact burned, too, in a far more bittersweet way. "I'm sorry about what happened earlier."

Ducking away from her touch, he gave a short bark

of laughter. "You're the only one who *doesn't* have a reason to apologize."

"Then please let me apologize on my friend's behalf." She sighed, her expression earnest. "Shane's a good guy, honestly."

Even as Gabe appreciated her loyalty, it stuck in his craw the way his fellow Mistletonians made excuses for each other, gave each other the benefit of the doubt. *Usually.*

"I hurt his feelings earlier this week," she added, "and he took it out on you."

Gabe didn't doubt she was telling the truth, but would McIntyre have behaved that way tonight if it had been anyone else shooting pool with Arianne? "He took it out on me because he doesn't like me."

"True." Arianne pursed her lips. "Which is weird because you're so warm, cuddly and lovable."

She'd gone from contrition to criticism? He clenched his truck keys in his fingers. "I don't need this."

"Are you sure?" she persisted. "Don't reach out to people because they deserve it—hell, maybe they don't—do it for yourself."

Who was she to dole out unsolicited advice? She'd obviously confused herself with a self-help guru. And confused him with someone who cared. "Good night, Arianne."

He stepped off the curb.

"Gabe?"

Against his better judgment, he turned. "Yes?" The single syllable held fourteen years of weariness.

She stood on her toes, sacrificing balance for height and letting herself stumble against him. His arms went around her reflexively. She placed a quick kiss just to the left of his mouth—if he turned his head a fraction of an inch, his lips could capture hers—and then stepped away.

"Thank you for a wonderful time," she said breathlessly.

Chapter Seven

"Brenna!" Arianne gratefully slowed to a walk. Her brother David swore that jogging was an excellent way to clear one's head and relieve stress. David was obviously out of his mind because she was every bit as tense as she had been when she'd climbed out of bed an hour ago. Plus, now her calves ached.

On the opposite sidewalk, local pet-sitter Brenna Pierce waved with her free hand. In her other, she held the handle of a double dog leash. Two dachshunds waddled out in front of her.

After a quick check for nonexistent traffic, Arianne crossed the street. "Good to see you. Have fun on your trip?"

The redhead grinned broadly from within her hoodie. "It was fantastic. Adam's kids are as great as he is. He and I will both be there tomorrow to help."

"Thanks, we can use the extra hands. Especially now." As the two women fell in step together, Arianne explained how they'd decided to add a partial pirate ship deck. And who would be building it.

"Gabriel Sloan, huh? Your influence," Brenna deduced.

"I did have something to do with it," Arianne admitted. The question was, would he honor the commitment she'd bullied him into accepting?

You don't know when to stop, David had once warned when she was younger. At the time, she was pretty sure her oh-so-mature response had been to stick out her tongue. Now she conceded that he had a point.

Why hadn't she allowed Gabe his dignified retreat last night? Or, having cornered him, why couldn't she simply have apologized for Shane's temporary idiocy and left it at that without lecturing? Of course, neither of those sins compared to the crowning audacity of kissing him good-night.

If she were going to scare him away from the festival for the sake of a kiss, she should have at least made it worth it. That reckless peck had done nothing more than whet an impossible appetite.

She covered her face with her hands and groaned behind her fingers.

"Problem?" Brenna asked, amusement lacing her curiosity. She stopped, letting the dogs sniff between a hydrangea bush and a Bradford pear tree.

Arianne took a deep breath. "Impulse control issues, a stubborn streak longer than the Chattahoochee, no common sense whatsoever… Take your pick."

"I wasn't going to pry, but does this have anything to do with some kind of commotion at On Tap? Adam and I dropped in for a drink after I'd done my final pet-sit for the night," Brenna admitted. "No one said anything directly to me, but I thought I overheard someone mention that you'd been there earlier on a date. With Gabe."

It was Mistletoe. People probably would have commented on Arianne being there with Gabe even without Shane's creating a scene. Still, she glanced skyward in the hope that maybe her family wouldn't hear any rumors about what had happened. She didn't want them interrogating her further about Gabe, nor did she want their friendships with Shane jeopardized over a lapse in judgment and one too many drink specials.

"*Commotion* might be a bit of an exaggeration," she objected. "*Date* isn't entirely accurate, either. We were both there playing pool with Quinn and Patrick Flannery, the new teacher at Whiteberry. Met him yet? He's a cutie."

"As cute as Gabe?" Brenna asked, thwarting the attempted subject change.

Gabe Sloan couldn't be cute even if he were wearing a pair of fuzzy bunny ears and held a baby in each arm. He was sexy and withdrawn and not currently a candidate for a healthy, romantic relationship. Arianne wanted to help him heal in any way she could, but she had too much self-preservation to date a guy that wounded.

"Patrick and Gabe are both good-looking in different ways," she said diplomatically. "So it's difficult to compare them."

"And you're sure you aren't dating Gabe?" Brenna asked.

Arianne laughed. "Wouldn't I know if I were?"

"Right. Sorry. It's just that you've made it clear that you find him attractive. Aren't you the same woman who counseled me over the summer that if you like a guy, you go out there and get him?"

Arianne opened her mouth to explain that it wasn't like that between her and Gabe. "I kissed him."

"Ha!" Brenna's exclamation got a companionable yip from one of the dogs. "Now that sounds more like the Arianne I know. Did he kiss you back?"

"It wasn't really that kind of kiss. Just a quick peck to end the evening."

"In other words, a traditional kiss good-night?" Brenna spared her the obvious statement that their evening sounded an awful lot like a date, but her expression spoke volumes. "You planning to kiss him again?"

"Definitely not."

Planning it? No.

Fantasizing about what it would be like if Gabe ever let himself get carried away, the sensation of having all that sensual intensity focused solely on her?

Well, that was a different story.

THERE WAS NOTHING more absurd than three large men who were waiting to pounce, trying to look inconspicuous.

As soon as Arianne entered the store, she spotted her brothers and father clumped around the register. The urge to spin on her heel and go right back the way she came was nearly overwhelming.

"Don't start," she cautioned.

Tanner had the gall to look puzzled. "Is that any way to greet your family? I, for one, don't even know what you're talking about."

Zachariah guffawed. "Nice try, son, but I raised her smarter than that. We wanted to talk to you, Ari."

Like this was a newsflash? "Do I get to at least take off my coat and pour some coffee before the Spanish Inquisition?"

"Is it true Shane and Gabe came to blows over you?" David asked, concern creasing his handsome face. "See whoever you like, but I want to know my little sister is safe and not dating some nut with a volatile temper."

"No one came to blows! Honestly. You know I love Mistletoe, but the local grapevine needs to simmer down." She shrugged out of her jacket and decided to go for that coffee. If they wanted to follow, fine, but she hadn't slept well and she wasn't postponing her caffeine fix to answer ludicrous allegations.

No one trailed her down the hall, but she couldn't stay in the back forever. She was officially on the clock and would need to open the store in ten minutes. Besides, since the topic had already been introduced, she wanted to find out exactly what was being spread around town.

"No punches were thrown," she reiterated when she returned. "Just some angry words. And Shane instigated those. Did the rumor mill manage to get that right?" Or were people who didn't have the facts blaming Gabe for events he hadn't caused?

"Shane picked a fight with Sloan?" David asked. "Not very bright."

"Actually, Shane picked a fight with *me*."

"Even less bright," Tanner said, a dangerous gleam in his light eyes. "Should we kick his ass?"

"Don't be ridiculous," Arianne said. "I don't need anyone riding to my rescue." She didn't plan ever to admit that there was a tiny, uncivilized part of her that had thrilled to the idea of Gabe physically defending her. Not that she needed to be protected from Shane.

"It wasn't that big a deal," she said. "Shane was upset over my rejecting him at the beginning of the week. Mix a bruised ego with a bad day and a few beers, you get one guy with a big mouth, casting aspersions on my taste in men and character in general."

Since she'd ruled out the bloodthirsty approach, David went for the pragmatic. "We can ban him from the store. No one talks to a Waide like that."

"What about a Sloan?" she mused, feeling that protective rush again, the one that made her want to take Gabe into her arms and soothe him with kisses. Except that her imagined scenario only remained soothing for about ten seconds before it blazed into something far more primal and far less altruistic.

"Huh?" Tanner asked. "What are you talking about?"

"You said no one talks to a Waide like that. What makes us special? You don't think Gabe deserves the same courtesy?"

The men exchanged glances, startled by her outburst.

"Never mind," she said. "I was just trying to make a hypothetical point. Can we get to work now?"

"You heard her," Zachariah said. "Let's get this place

open for business. That Alaskan cruise your mother wants to take isn't going to pay for itself."

Arianne smiled gratefully at her father. He and David went in the back to switch the phone from its prerecorded message over to live calls and get things up and running in the office. Tanner gathered up his coat and briefcase, preparing to go.

"Bye, shortie." He ruffled her hair, but then stood there, searching her face instead of leaving.

"I'm fine," she said through her teeth. "Just annoyed at Shane's macho proprietary B.S. He had no right to treat Gabe like that."

Tanner laughed. "My guess is that Gabe can take care of himself."

He shouldn't have to. No one should go through life alone, she thought, wildly grateful that she hadn't been an only child. Gabe's mother had died during his childhood, and she didn't think his father had remarried. Were both Sloan men lonely? Maybe she shouldn't worry so much about helping him reconnect with the random and assorted citizens of Mistletoe and simply help him build a stronger relationship with his dad. She couldn't imagine where she'd be without her own family.

She made shooing motions toward the door. "Be gone already."

"Okay. But I'll be back. This conversation isn't necessarily over."

"You mean, you're going to be obnoxious about this?"

"Put yourself in my shoes," he said. "If you were

worried about me or David, would you leave us alone to muddle through it ourselves or butt in with nosy questions and blunt advice?"

Arianne sighed. "That's what I was afraid of."

GABE WORKED FEVERISHLY on Friday morning, trying to squeeze an entire day's productivity into half his normal hours…and trying to take his mind off Arianne's surprising exit last night. He thought he'd be the one to walk away, yet she'd kissed him, then disappeared back inside before he could even process what had happened.

A wonderful time, she'd said. Which part? His being socially awkward with her, nearly decking a friend of hers or leaving without a proper goodbye?

Admit it, you were having a good time, too. Before Shane's interruption, Gabe had enjoyed shooting pool, bantering with Arianne.

He worked through his normal lunch hour, then called it a day around two o'clock, wanting the afternoon to explore new opportunities. At home he put in calls to a distant cousin and to Mike, letting them know he'd appreciate it if they kept their ears to the ground regarding job openings or reasonably priced housing. He even phoned Nicole Jones, although he experienced an irrational slash of guilt when he heard her voice.

Arianne's face flashed in his mind, which made him gruff when he answered Nicole's delighted greeting.

"It's been too long since we talked," Nicole scolded. "You know, Atlanta's not that far away, if you ever want to get away for a weekend."

There was a time when he would have taken her up on what she was offering. He'd met Nicole last year, when she'd been a recent divorcée on temporary leave from her law firm and in town to restore and sell the house her great-aunt had left her. She'd hired Gabe and they'd hit it off almost immediately. They'd both known from the onset that it would be a brief affair— she was still going through the grieving process for her marriage—but he'd never regretted the time they spent together.

Talking to her now, he suspected that they'd only be platonic friends going forward. He felt no spark of desire. "Actually, Nic, what I want is to get away permanently. I'm job-hunting. Can I use you as a reference?"

"Absolutely! You probably doubled what I would have made on that house."

They talked for a few minutes, and it was comfortable. Like a flannel shirt. Nothing like the prickly, charged encounters he had with Arianne.

Damn it. What was that, the fiftieth time he'd thought of her today? Determined to put her out of his mind, he booted up his computer, checking a few occupational sites and tweaking his résumé. As he surfed some job postings, he had an idea. What if he found a college campus that had open positions in the grounds crew or repair and maintenance? Did university employees get discounts on tuition? Once upon a time, he'd planned to take classes, get a degree. Sure, he was older than the typical freshman, but maybe it wasn't too late.

If he were going to be taken seriously as an applicant

anywhere, however, he would need more references than Nicole Jones. He would have to ask some people from Mistletoe. He decided to start with Mindy Nelson, a widow who not only hired Gabe regularly, but who'd told him once that her brother-in-law, owner of a small residential construction company in Florida, had been impressed with the deck Gabe had built for her.

Mindy worked over at the Mistletoe senior center. Gabe looked up the number in the phone book and called.

"Mindy Nelson," she chirped.

"Hi, it's Gabe Sloan—"

"Gabriel! I was just talking about you. Dele Momsen and I had lunch together and she told me about how you're helping with her walk-the-plank idea. I'm sure you'll do a wonderful job. I've always been so impressed with your work."

He blinked at the effusive praise. "Thank you, ma'am. That makes what I called you about a little easier. I'm interested in pursuing other career possibilities and wondered if I could list you as a—"

"Oh, where are you interviewing?"

"Nowhere yet. I'm putting together applications."

"For places in town?" she asked, sounding confused. "Will you still have your own business on the side?"

"Actually, I want to look outside Mistletoe. I think it's time for me to move on."

"What? Oh, no! We'll hate to see you go."

He doubted many people would share that sentiment, but he was touched nonetheless. "I'll miss you, too. You're one of my favorite customers."

"I don't suppose that if I withheld my recommendation we'd get to keep you?"

He laughed at the possibility of Mindy Nelson, who couldn't even kill a bug—he'd seen her catch them in jars to release outside—scheming to keep him from leaving. "No, I'm definitely going some time after the fall festival." Wouldn't it be nice to move over the winter and be settled before January? A new life in the new year. *Perfect.*

"I suppose I'm morally obligated," she grumbled. "A man with a work ethic like yours deserves all the praise he can get. But I'm not happy about this!"

After a moment's debate, he decided to press his luck. "Then would I be completely insensitive to ask you for your brother-in-law's contact information? I've never really pictured myself living in Florida, but who knows? Maybe the Sunshine State would be the perfect place for me."

"Maybe," she said slowly. "I'll call him this weekend and put in a good word for you. I can't guarantee he's hiring, but he has nothing to lose by talking to you."

"Thank you," he said sincerely. "I can't tell you how much I appreciate this. Have a good weekend, Mrs. Nelson."

"You, too. Oh, and, Gabriel? Don't you pay any mind to that Shane McIntyre. I know his mom, and he was a good kid, but always been something of a hothead. Anyone with half a brain can see Arianne's not right for him, but I suppose he'll just have to figure that out for himself. It'll blow over."

"I… Thanks," he said lamely. He told himself he was used to being at the center of Mistletoe gossip, but maybe you never truly adjusted to being the center of other people's conversations—the uncomfortable scrutiny, the half-truths.

He was hardly astonished to discover that news of last night's argument was making the rounds, but he *was* pleasantly surprised to find someone had taken his side.

Chapter Eight

Gabe supposed the main problem with volunteers was that they were, by definition, not professionals. For a man who worked alone and knew the name and function of pretty much every power tool on the market, Saturday morning was a bit too chaotic. A couple dozen well-meaning people—many with children in tow—milled around with only a limited idea of what they should be doing.

Thankfully that lasted for only a short while before Quinn and Lilah herded everyone into the impromptu headquarters they'd set up in the town square gazebo. Even among the crush of bodies beneath the gazebo roof, Gabe was continuously aware of Arianne's location. He could pick her voice out of the cacophony, could feel whenever she looked in his direction. He assiduously did not look in hers. She would say that he was avoiding her, accuse him of running away again in a more subtle form.

Damn straight he planned to avoid her! He was willing to build an entire pirate armada in return for Arianne not kissing him again. Because if she tried, he would succumb to temptation. He'd spent too many unguarded moments since Thursday night imagining the taste of her, the softness of her lips beneath his, her skin against his. He was reputed to be someone who gave in to baser instincts with no thought for consequences. If Arianne got too close, he'd end up proving his fabled lack of self-control.

In the center of the gazebo, Lilah and Quinn mapped out where everything would be—various midway games down Main Street, arts and crafts booths on the courthouse lawn, concessions scattered throughout, a large rock-climbing wall in the post-office parking lot.

A freckled boy sitting not far from Gabe leaned forward at the mention of the climbing wall. "I'm gonna do it this year!"

An older boy with similar features shoved the child's shoulder. "You've been saying that for two years, Ben. Face it, you're a big fraidy cat, scared of heights. You're never gonna climb that wall."

"I am, too, Toby!" But the youngster's lower lip trembled.

Gabe sighed inwardly. *Chin up, kid.* Crying would only be taken as an additional sign of cowardice.

"Ben! Toby!" A woman with strawberry blond hair shushed them, and Lilah and Quinn began sending volunteers off with specific assignments. They'd restored order admirably well, and Gabe hoped he could get to work soon on erecting the plank platform, left more or less alone.

He hadn't even reached the site Lilah had designated, the small gravel lot next to the library, before someone approached. Jack Allen. A sour taste rose in Gabe's mouth. Jack worked as an administrator for the town of Mistletoe and was the younger brother of someone Gabe had beat to a near pulp in high school.

"Hey, Gabe," Jack called.

He sounded a lot like his brother actually. *Hey, Gabe.*

As if it had been yesterday, Gabe could hear Duke Allen in his head.

Wait up.

Warily, Gabe's sophomore self had turned, wondering if yet another person was about to insinuate that he was responsible for two deaths. Three, if one counted the mother he'd never known.

But Duke Allen had beamed at him. *I know you're taking a lot of flack, dude, but I'm on your side. Who wouldn't have bagged Mrs. Templeton, given the chance? I gotta know, was she as hot in bed as I think?*

The memory blurred after that, ending with the principal and vice principal separating them and the look of contempt in Jeremy Sloan's eyes when he'd come to pick up his suspended son.

Gabe swallowed. "Jack."

"Quinn said I should see you about the ladder?"

"What? Oh, the ladder. Yeah. Follow me to my truck." Gabe had offered the use of his commercial-grade ladder, knowing it extended well beyond the ladders most people had at home.

"I couldn't make the meeting the other night," Jack

said. "Zoning commission meeting ran late. But I wanted to add that I think the pirate ship idea is a nice touch. We appreciate your taking time out of your schedule to put it together so quickly."

From someone else, the remark could have been snide, a pointed reminder that Gabe didn't have much of a social schedule. But Jack was completely amiable. If he recalled Gabe's regrettably lost temper in high school, he wasn't holding a grudge.

When they reached the truck, Gabe said, "This ladder's pretty heavy. Where are you headed with it?"

"Just around the corner, to Butler Street. We're raising the big bingo tent and stringing up the speakers."

The two of them carried the ladder together. Jack said that when he was done with it, he and someone else would bring it to Gabe, who would need it this afternoon.

Not five minutes later, Gabe was hailed again. This time by Tanner Waide. Gabe could guess what the man wanted to discuss. *Arianne, what trouble have you got me into now?* The idea of defending himself with the God's honest truth—that *she* had made the move on *him*—was enticing, but he discounted it as ungallant. Besides, in his experience, people rarely believed that explanation.

"Tanner, what can I do for you?" he asked, slowing his gait but not stopping.

"I don't need anything." The man smiled, heightening his familial resemblance to Arianne. "Actually I came to say that if there's anything you ever need…"

When Tanner broke off with a frown, Gabe found

himself confused. "You mean, like assistance with the pirate ship?"

"Not exactly. Although I'd be happy to help." Tanner rubbed his jaw. "This is more awkward than I'd intended, but I heard about the confrontation with Shane."

Gabe sighed. Would Arianne's brother believe him if he explained that he wasn't looking for any trouble?

"I just want you to know we've got your back."

"Excuse me?"

"David and me. If you want us to correct any misconceptions about how it went down. Or if you think Shane's not getting the message about Ari not being interested, I'd appreciate your letting me know. I'll have a chat with him."

Gabe's gaze went involuntarily to Tanner's hand, and the other man noticed, chuckling.

"That wasn't a euphemism for roughing him up. He's known the family for years, and we owe it to him to try talking first if his behavior's become inappropriate." Tanner's expression suddenly hardened. "Unless he ever lays a hand on my little sister, in which case I'll dump his body in the river."

If Shane hurt Ari in front of Gabe, Tanner would never get the chance to kill him. Gabe didn't voice the thought—it seemed risky, given his history and the fact that three local police officers were helping with the huge canvas bingo tent. But some of the protective ferocity he was feeling must have shown in his expression because Tanner rocked back on the balls of his feet, looking satisfied.

"I see we're in agreement," Tanner said. "I'll let you get back to work, then. But we'll have a beer soon so I can give you advice."

"Advice?" What had he done to make the Waides think they were his own personal consulting team?

"On how to manage my sister."

"I don't think that's possible," Gabe grumbled.

Tanner grinned. "You're a quick learner."

GABE PAUSED, WIPING his forehead with the back of his arm. He was mighty glad they'd asked for his help with the fall festival and not the July Fourth celebration. Even with the cool October air, he was working up a sweat. He set the hammer he'd been using across the top of his toolbox and reached for a bottle of water. It had long since turned lukewarm, but at least it was wet.

He stood and twisted off the lid, gratefully rehydrating.

"I feel bad that I didn't think to bring you another bottle. You look like you're about out," Lilah observed as she emerged from a shaded trail between two buildings.

"That's okay." He crumpled the plastic to stick it in the recycling bin. "I'll probably head for lunch soon anyway, so I can get something else to drink then."

"Could you hold off on that lunch for another fifteen minutes?" she asked. "Jennifer Gideon just handed me the check from the PTA and the bouncy company is supposed to be delivering the ball pit back here. Can you direct them, let them know exactly where you need it?"

"Sure." He smiled. "But if I pass out from hunger in the meantime, it's on your head."

She looked startled for a second and he wondered if she'd taken him seriously, but then she gave a little shake of her head. "After the diving pit is set up, why don't you come to lunch with us? Tanner and I were talking about going for Mexican."

"You do know I was kidding about the fainting?"

"That's what I figured. I just thought it would be nice if you could join us." She hesitated before adding, "Ari will be there."

If he were a smarter man, that would be a reason *not* to go. Hadn't he been thinking to himself that the more distance between them, the better? But…

He missed her smile. In retrospect, he'd been braced all morning for her to seek him out, to interrupt, and now that she hadn't, the relief he should be feeling was tainted with disappointment.

"She's trying to give you space," Lilah said in a near whisper, glancing around as if nervous she would be caught betraying a confidence. "She's afraid she comes on too strong."

She does. So why wasn't he happier that she was staying away?

"It won't last," Lilah predicted. "She's trying to back off because she's told herself she *should,* but it's too contrary to her nature. The Waides are strong-willed."

"Including your husband?"

Lilah laughed. "Especially my husband! Don't let the aw-shucks twinkle in his eyes or easy smile fool you.

You should have seen the full-court press I got when he moved back to Mistletoe. I was afraid he could break my heart again and wanted nothing to do with him."

Gabe pointed to the wedding band she wore. "Looks like he wore you down."

"Put that way, it doesn't sound very romantic, huh?" She wrinkled her nose. "But trust me, even though I thought he was going to drive me crazy at the time, letting myself love him was the best decision I ever made."

A truck parked at the curb and a couple of guys crunched across the gravel to ask if she was Lilah and if this was where the ball pit would go. Nodding, she introduced them to Gabe. He took it from there and she excused herself to go check on the progress with the bingo tent and midway facade.

"Think about that lunch offer," she reminded him over her shoulder.

He grinned at her retreating back—Lilah was a bit like her relentless sister-in-law, she was just more understated about it.

Together the three men got the "mega pit" situated and inflated the base to determine whether this was going to work safely. When Gabe was satisfied that walking the plank would be a lighthearted fundraiser and not a short plummet into traction, he thanked the uniformed men and signed the paperwork saying that he understood the safety regulations and instructions for how to use the electric blower. They unloaded seven enormous bags filled with springy, multicolored balls. As he handed over the clipboard, he caught sight of a paint-smeared blonde and two kids in his peripheral vision.

Arianne. She was crouched down in the picturesque pathway that led between the buildings and back toward Main Street. Her hair was pulled back with some kind of clip, but long strands were blowing around her face as she crouched next to two kids. It looked as though she was mediating an argument between the two ginger-haired boys Gabe had seen in the gazebo earlier. Gabe started walking toward them even before he realized that was his intention.

"Everything okay here?" he asked. At least if he sounded as if he were trying to help, he wouldn't have to admit to himself that, having finally seen her, he couldn't stay away.

"It will be," Arianne said. Her stern tone was full of warning, but Gabe wondered if the blue smear of paint across her left cheek detracted from her authority. "Right, guys?"

The youngest—seven, maybe?—nodded, sniffling, and the taller one kicked the dirt with his shoe as he muttered an unconvincing, "Yes, ma'am."

"Why don't the two of you go help Quinn clean paintbrushes?" she suggested. "Your mom said as soon as she's done, she'll take you to lunch at the Dixieland Diner. Play your cards right, there might even be milk shakes in your future."

Their expressions brightening slightly at the implied bribe, they scampered off and disappeared around the corner of the bank.

"You think they're really on their way to assist Quinn?" Gabe asked. Neither child had looked particularly eager to tackle that errand.

Arianne sighed. "Who knows? Toby and Ben are good kids, for the most part, but a handful for Fawne. Her husband is serving a tour of duty overseas. She's here instead of on a base because she's trying to help take care of her parents, and it's a lot on her plate."

Gabe stared off in the direction the boys had gone. "I don't want them operating power saws or hammering a platform that needs to hold actual festival attendees without collapsing, but if I rack my brain, I might be able to come up with something they can do to help me."

"Really? My hero." Her radiant smile made him feel he was strong enough to stop a speeding locomotive. Or run faster than a speeding locomotive. Definitely something in the locomotive genre.

Embarrassed by the swell of pride he felt at her reaction, he downplayed his generosity. "It's not that big a deal. Patrick and Lilah and Quinn deal with entire classrooms full of kids on a daily basis. Seems like a minor enough task for me to keep two of them out of trouble for an hour or so."

"It will be a big deal to *them*," she protested. "Getting to hang out with a big strong guy and build stuff when their own father is so far away, instead of trailing after their mom all afternoon? I know having them underfoot will probably slow you down, and you're sweet to offer."

Sweet? Gabe wasn't sure whether to be amused by the unlikely adjective or vaguely offended.

"So, what have you been working on all morning?" he asked casually. "I assume paint was involved."

He brushed his thumb over a smudge of yellow on the inside of her elbow. She trembled. He wished she hadn't. Her natural responsiveness made her even more irresistible.

"Headless bodies," she said.

Gabe raised an eyebrow at her unexpectedly gruesome answer. "I don't follow."

"Waide Supply donated large pieces of plywood and the school's art teacher drew silly outlines. The kind you stick your head through for photo ops. A few of us have been painting them. She's got one of a pirate captain to put near your ship.

"Speaking of which…" she said, sounding uncharacteristically shy.

It was endearing to see an alternate side of her, but made him realize he'd grown to genuinely like her brash confidence.

"Yes?" he prompted.

"How's progress on your ship going?" she asked. "I'd be happy to round up some volunteers or even pitch in myself. Although, last time I offered, you questioned my construction skills. And I…didn't want to be pushy."

Her confession unbalanced him. Despite his previous complaints, it seemed inherently wrong that Arianne should try to be anything other than the strong, sexy, surprising woman she was.

"You are who you are." It came out clumsily, not nearly encompassing how much he admired her.

"Is that your fatalistic way of saying I'm doomed to keep making the same mistakes?"

"No!" He cupped her chin, tilting her head up. "No, it's my way of…" There were a half a dozen things he could tell her, except he couldn't find the right words to articulate any of them.

Maybe he should try action instead.

His heart raced with the anticipation that had been escalating since she'd brushed her lips across his skin the other night. That whisper of a caress had teased at the corners of his imagination for the past two days, stoking an undeniable craving. Arianne's lips parted, and her eyes closed as he bent toward her. For reasons known only to herself, Arianne seemed to believe in him, and he should probably repay that with a gentleman's kiss, soft and slow-building. Respectful.

Instead, Gabe kissed her like the town bad boy he was. Hungry and hard, pressing his open mouth to hers and sinking into the warmth of her.

She clutched the front of his shirt. He wasn't sure if she was trying to pull him even closer or holding on to him for balance. There was a bench behind them, and he moved them in that direction until the back of his legs bumped iron. Then he sat, tugging Arianne with him. She wasn't quite in his lap, but so tantalizingly close that need roared through him.

Fragmented thoughts circled like distant birds high above, little more than indistinguishable *M*'s against the clouds. *Public place. Shouldn't. She deserves…*

But Arianne tunneled her hands through his hair and

slid her tongue against his, obliterating the paltry objections his rational mind posed. She was soft and hot in his arms, and he let his hand drop from her shoulder to her blouse, over the fullness of her breast.

Push my hand away. One of them needed to be sane.

Arianne groaned his name and arched into him.

Hell, sanity was overrated anyway.

It took him a moment to realize that the feminine gasp he heard had not come from the beautiful woman kissing him.

Then Lilah's voice boomed at them, unnaturally loud in the clearing. "You know what, honey? I just realized I left my keys over at the bingo tent. Would you mind going back to get them?"

Even though most of the blood had left Gabe's brain, he had the wherewithal to gently push Arianne aside. She was straightening her paint-stained button-down shirt and looked nearly composed by the time Lilah reached them. Gabe kept his gaze averted, breathing hard. It would be a few seconds before he could function like a normal human being again.

"Sorry to interrupt," Lilah said, sounding far too delighted to be truly penitent. "Tanner and I were coming to see if Gabe would join us for lunch."

"You Waides," Gabe drawled. "You just don't give up."

"One of our numerous fantastic attributes," Lilah agreed. "Also, many of us are good kissers, but I see you've discovered that for yourself."

"Li-*lah!*"

Arianne's squeak of protest left her sister-in-law unfazed.

"Couldn't help myself." Lilah chuckled. "Think back to how often you've teased me and Tanner over the years. Do you know how many times you walked in on us necking back when we were teenagers?"

"Of course I know. Seeing my *brother* in a hot clinch?" Arianne exaggerated a shudder. "Those incidents scarred me for life."

If Lilah hadn't found an excuse to send her husband away before he'd gotten an eyeful, Gabe had a feeling he would currently be maimed for life. Not fully meeting her eyes, he offered a heartfelt, "Thank you."

He could hear the smile in her voice. "So, about lunch?"

A frigid, ice-cold shower sounded like a much better idea than sitting next to Arianne for the next forty minutes, trying to act as if he didn't want to drag her off to bed while her brother watched from the other side of the table. "Um…"

Arianne covered his hand with hers. "Please, Gabe?"

He felt himself drowning in her eyes and didn't mind. Who needed air? "All right. But I need to do something about the balls first."

Arianne's eyebrows shot up, and Gabe gave a strangled laugh. "For the pit. Remember? Big container people are going to walk into? The company delivered our supplies, and aside from the base, I don't want to just leave everything out."

"Of course." Her face pinkened, and she busied herself with reclipping her hair. "I knew what you were talking about."

"I need to get my toolbox, too." Would all seven bags even fit in his truck? "We're going to need a good-sized storage space to keep all the bags. Unless we want to divvy them up among us?"

Lilah shook her head. "No, even with the advance prep, next Saturday will be hectic. Keeping everything together will make it go more smoothly. We can store the balls in the guest room at my house. We only use it when we have—"

"Sweetheart?" Tanner called. "I didn't see your keys."

She turned with a guileless smile that made Gabe think she deserved an acting award. "Sorry about that, hon. They turned out to be in my pocket."

Tanner narrowed his eyes, well aware that his wife wasn't a ditz but not pressing her for a better explanation. "Well, I'm starving. Are we ready to go or what?"

"Just about," Gabe said, standing. "Can you help me carry some bags to my truck? They aren't too heavy, just cumbersome. Once we get those and my tools secured, we can go."

"Anything to speed this along," Tanner said affably, following Gabe toward the clearing that spilled out into the gravel lot.

"We'll be along in just a second," Lilah said, tossing a friendly arm around Arianne's shoulders. It occurred to Gabe that he was about to be the topic of conversation. From years of habit, he bristled at the idea. He liked flying below the social radar. *Then you should refrain from publicly mauling the daughter of a community pillar.*

As he came around the corner of the library, Gabe noticed that his ladder was propped against the back of an antiques store opposite them. It had probably been returned from the front of the lot because the path between buildings was too narrow to maneuver well, thank God, or Gabe and Arianne— There was a split-second delay between seeing the fifteen-foot ladder and realizing that there was a kid climbing it.

Ben. The little boy who was afraid of heights.

Chapter Nine

Gabe's instinct was to cross the lot at a run, but he didn't want to startle the kid into falling. The ladder was merely resting there, not safely grounded on the uneven gravel for actual use. Cold fear gripped Gabe. *He could break his neck.*

He and Tanner exchanged stricken looks.

"Go get help," Gabe instructed, not caring what form that help took as long as they got this kid down safely. Were there still firemen at the bingo tent, or had they gone to lunch? Did they have nets and safety equipment with them, or were they stored at the fire station?

He walked purposefully toward the kid, noticing as he went that the ladder was shaking. The little boy, who'd nearly reached the top, was crying.

"Ben?" Gabe called softly. "You're okay, buddy."

"No, I'm n-not. I'm afraid just l-like my br-br—"

They could address phobias and self-esteem and *not climbing ladders unsupervised* later. Right now, Gabe needed to reach the kid before the whole damn thing fell over.

"Hold on."

But the child wasn't listening. His pitiful little howls were gathering strength, and Gabe heard Arianne's sharp intake of breath behind him as Ben reflexively lifted a hand to wipe his nose. Gabe dived for the tilting ladder as it scraped against the side of the building. Ben shrieked.

Gabe didn't have time to steady it, not with Ben's shaky weight working against him. "Just let go, buddy. I'll catch you." Please, God, let his words be true.

Instead, Ben panicked and scrambled to get down, further upsetting the ladder. As it started to topple, he either decided to trust Gabe or just plain lost his grip. He smashed down into Gabe's chest. Gabe staggered back, tightening his hold to keep the kid safe, barely able to register the discomfort in his rib cage before a much more powerful blow struck him across the skull.

Tanner tried to help him into a sitting position as Arianne pulled Ben into her waiting arms. There was a ringing so intense in Gabe's ears that the sound nauseated him, but somewhere beyond it, he focused on Arianne's low, soothing voice. He thought he heard her say that Lilah had gone to find Ben's mom.

"Sh-she'll be mad," the boy fretted. "I was supposed to stay with Toby, but I wanted to prove I was brave. Like m-my daddy." The last word ended on a wail that was like a machete to Gabe's temple.

"Benjamin August Harris!"

Gabe's stomach lurched. Must everyone yell? Suddenly Arianne appeared in the halo of his blurred vision.

"Are you all right? How many fingers am I holding up?"

He tried to focus on her hand. Eleven? That couldn't be right. "Don't worry. Hardheaded. Like you." To prove his point and erase the fear pinching her face, he lurched to his feet.

And the world went temporarily dark.

GABE WAS OUT ONLY a moment, but apparently when you were dealing with women, that was more than enough time for them to conclude you had to go to the hospital.

"You blacked out!" Arianne said, blessedly keeping her voice soft despite her vehemence.

"Just stood too fast," he mumbled. "Aspirin, bed, be fine." Aspirin, a few hours rest and plenty of time in bed with *her,* he'd be even better. But he lacked the energy to invite her to kiss and make it better.

Meanwhile, Fawne Harris was gushing to the rapidly gathering crowd that Gabe had saved her son. Everyone parted to make way for the red truck. Tanner had taken Gabe's keys and gone to get his vehicle so that he didn't have to walk all the way between buildings and across lots to where he'd parked.

Tanner stepped out of the truck and tossed the keys to Arianne.

"You want Lilah and me to come with you?" her brother asked.

"I've got it from here," Arianne said. She sounded almost like a protective mama bear.

It made Gabe smile, the crazy idea of the tiny woman

shielding him from danger, but moving his facial muscles only added to the agony in his head. So he gave up arguing and let Lilah and Tanner help him into the passenger seat of his truck.

Once he was buckled, he told Arianne, "Never let a woman drive it before."

"Don't worry, David taught me to drive stick when I was still in high school. Close your eyes and leave the ride to me."

Luckily, business in the E.R. was slow this afternoon, and the doctor saw Gabe pretty quickly. He asked him some questions and did a rudimentary exam before concluding, "MTBI."

"What's that?" Arianne asked, sounding alarmed. Gabe wanted to hug her, to reassure her that he was all right, but it was difficult to portray unharmed strength when the room tilted every time he moved.

"A concussion," the doctor explained.

Well, duh. Gabe figured everyone who'd been in town square with them, right down to little Ben, could have made that diagnosis and spared him the extra stop at the hospital with all its painfully bright fluorescent lights overhead.

He swallowed, squinting at the doctor. "Can I have some aspirin?"

"Not for a concussion! Acetaminophen would be better. I'll get you some of that." The man turned to Arianne. "Can you or someone else keep an eye on him for the next twenty-four hours? He should make a follow-up appointment for Monday, but in the mean-

time, if he gets worse, you should bring him back in."
He gave her some symptoms to watch for, like vomiting
and growing confusion.

Earlier that afternoon, the idea of Arianne spending
the night with him would have sounded like paradise,
but not in his current condition. Gabe felt woozy and
vulnerable and not a little foolish, getting conked on the
head with his own damn ladder.

"Feeling better," he lied to her as she navigated the
labyrinth of the hospital's parking garage to get them
back out on the main road. "You don't have to stay once
you drop me off."

"I don't mind," she said firmly.

I do.

She slanted him a sidelong look. "All right, how
about I call your father?"

"What?" He hadn't meant to yell. Damn, that hurt.

"You were just in the hospital. Even if you don't ask
him to come over, shouldn't we at least call your dad to
notify him?"

"*At* the hospital, not in," Gabe differentiated. "And, no."

"I thought maybe you'd be more comfortable with a
parent taking care of you instead of me."

Throughout Gabe's life, his father had made him feel
guilty, had made him feel unloved and had made him
itch to leave home. But made him comfortable? No.
That was not in Jeremy's repertoire.

"Is there…" She hesitated. "Is there anyone else
you'd like me to call, then? To watch over you?"

Either the acetaminophen was kicking in or his body

was simply shutting down as a defense mechanism against the throbbing pain, because the earlier excruciating agony was giving way to a duller, achy sleepiness. Was there anyone else he'd rather be with than Arianne, anyone else he trusted more in this situation?

"Stay." His eyes closed. "Stay with me."

EVEN ASLEEP, GABE DIDN'T look at peace. Arianne parked the truck beneath the carport outside the old Mitchell barn. It was no secret Gabe had bought the place and had been slowly fixing it up; she'd wondered several times over the past few weeks what the interior of his home looked like. Now she'd get an insider's view. She felt a dash of shame over her curiosity—the man was hurt! This was no time to be thinking of herself. But then she forgave herself. After all, who could blame a girl for wanting to learn more about the man she was…

Falling for? Lusting after? Thinking about on an hourly basis?

"Gabe." She nudged his shoulder. Not being able to wake a person up could be a sign that the concussion was more severe than first realized. But she had no frame of reference. How difficult was Gabe to wake up normally? What if he was like Tanner, who slept like the dead?

At least Gabe mumbled something, so she knew he'd heard her.

She gave it another shot. "C'mon, big guy. We're home, and I need your help. I can shoot pool with the boys, drive a stick shift and occasionally cuss like a sailor, but lifting you is beyond even my capabilities."

Though he groused incoherently the entire time, he managed to slide out of the truck. She put her arm around his waist and looped his arm around her neck. Was she a terrible person for noticing the sculpted definition of his muscles at a time like this?

She found the house key on the ring in her hand and unlocked the door. There weren't an abundance of windows, and she reached automatically for a light switch, but Gabe emitted a low whimpering sound that made her rethink that. Was there enough illumination that she could help him down the hall to his room without walking into a wall or tripping over something?

"Can you make it to the bed?" she asked.

He glanced at her and, despite the pain etched around his eyes, smiled. "Dare you to ask me that another time."

Desire pierced her. He'd sustained a concussion saving a little boy and *still* had the stamina to flirt with her? At this rate, he'd ruin her for other men.

She stiffened at the thought. Even though it had been partially flippant, there was a kernel of actual risk there. Every man she'd ever dated had been from Mistletoe and she couldn't imagine getting swept away with any of them the way she had with Gabe on that bench.

Either because he was feeling better now that he was in dimmer surroundings or because sheer masculine pride forbade him from continuing to lean on her, Gabe led the way to his room. Her passing impression was that the former barn was sectioned into thirds, with a high-ceilinged living room in the middle and a kitchen and bedroom on the ends.

She found his bed in the same state as hers—sloppily made. It made Arianne feel like too much of a slob to leave her sheets and blankets twisted any which way when she left home for the day, but she didn't bother with a lot of tucking and creasing or pillow arranging. She sidestepped him and pulled down the corner of a forest-green comforter. There was a large picture window in here, but the shade was drawn behind tan-and-green curtains.

He sat on the edge of the bed, his eyes at half-mast.

Arianne knew that if she offered her help, he'd turn it down, so instead of asking, she simply knelt and pulled off the hiking boots he wore. "You lie down," she instructed in her best no-nonsense tone. "Is there anything I can get you?" It was too soon for any more medicine. She tried to think what would possibly make her feel better if she'd had a seventy-pound kid fall into her, followed by a ladder hurtling down on her head.

She shook her head, trying to dislodge the morbid what-ifs. "You really were quite the hero today." Ben could easily have ended his day with broken bones, or worse if he'd fallen at the wrong angle. Then there was the possibility that he could have been injured in a fall and again when the ladder crashed atop him.

Gabe closed his eyes, his voice a tired slur. "Had to. Can't take a fourth death on my head."

Fourth? Arianne recoiled in surprise. Who, besides the Templetons, did he obviously blame himself for? Now didn't seem like an appropriate time to ask.

"Arianne? Could you bring an ice pack?"

"Of course." Arianne was a doer by nature. She was relieved to have a specific and helpful task.

In the kitchen, she flipped on the light and saw a suite of silver appliances, including a flat-range stove and a trash compactor. Crossing to the three-door refrigerator, she decided that the freezer compartment was probably the one with the ice dispenser. She opened the door and stared.

"Good Lord, it looks like he robbed the Breckfield Creamery."

She'd never seen so much ice cream in one person's kitchen. Individual servings and pints of exotic flavors inside the door, half gallons of country-style vanilla and mint-chocolate chip sharing a shelf, and boxes of individually wrapped ice-cream sandwiches. He must exert a *lot* of physical effort on the job to maintain a body that looked like his. Even though she knew there was no valid logic to her impromptu reasoning, she wished the more suspicious-minded citizens of Mistletoe could see the contents of his freezer. The man owned a tiny pink carton of Bubble Gum Bliss, for crying out loud—how evil could he be?

Realizing that she was taking her time snooping while the hero of the day was still lying in agony, she jerked her attention away from all the frozen dairy goodness and found a blue gel pack. The sudden ring of a phone splintering the silence nearly made her jump. After only two rings—Arianne had programmed hers to five in case she had trouble finding the cordless—Gabe's voice rumbled from the answering machine on the tiled kitchen counter.

"You've reached Sloan Carpentry and Odd Jobs. Leave a message at the beep or, in case of emergency, page my cell."

Right after he gave the number for that, a woman spoke. "It's Nicole. I may have an idea for a job possibility if you're willing to move to Kennesaw. Give me a call if you want more details—it was great to hear from you the other day."

Nicole? Against her will, Arianne recalled what Shane had told her. *Kitchen tile wasn't all he laid for Nicole Jones.*

Even if Shane was right, what business was it of Arianne's? Every adult had a romantic past. No, the pang she suffered probably wasn't jealousy over a woman with whom Gabe may have once been involved, a woman who no longer even lived in Mistletoe. Instead, Arianne suspected that the reason it temporarily hurt to breathe was because even though Gabe had told her point-blank that he planned to leave, she'd harbored the subconscious hope that he'd change his mind.

She shot the answering machine a malevolent glare. Good thing she wasn't a selfish, devious person or that message might accidentally get erased before Gabe was fully recovered. Pretending she was too noble to have even had such a thought, she left the kitchen and hurried down the hall.

Gabe wasn't snoring, but his breathing was audible, deep and even. She crept forward, figuring she could leave the ice pack on the nightstand in case his headache woke him up in the immediate future. Unable to resist the temptation of studying him at her leisure, she sat gently on the edge of the bed. Gabriel. It was a fitting name for him. He was formed beautifully enough to look like an angel, albeit one with the weight of the world on his broad shoulders.

As she gazed down at him—this six-foot loner with surprise dimples and a secret love for ice cream— tenderness swamped her.

She bent to graze his forehead with a featherlight kiss. Unexpectedly, the arm at his side clamped around her, drawing her inexorably to him. He never even opened his eyes.

"Gabe?" she whispered.

Nothing.

She was squashed into his torso and had to wiggle around so she could breathe easier and so that she wasn't lying in such a way that pulled her long hair. His breathing was still relaxed, but his arm was like an iron band around her. She debated the best way to slip loose without disturbing his well-earned rest. *Oh, heck with it.* Despite his teasing remark about taking her to bed earlier, who knew if she'd ever have this chance again?

Deciding to enjoy it while she was here, she tucked her chin against his chest and succumbed to the luxury of being in Gabe's arms.

Chapter Ten

When Gabe woke in the dark room, his head hurt some but it was a distant pain that paled in comparison to the other physical sensations jolting his body. Arianne was snuggled across him, her warm weight draped over him like the world's sexiest blanket, her thigh pressing against his erection. Although he wasn't complaining, he couldn't remember crawling into bed with her.

He barely recalled finding the grit to make it down the hall on his own two feet. How long had they been here? No light shone around the edges of the window shade, so the sun must have already set. To get a look at the digital clock on his dresser he would have to shift Arianne, and he didn't want to disturb her.

In fact, part of him wanted nothing more than to sink back into slumber, enjoying her nearness and accepting it as fate's gift to him, a reward for helping that kid earlier. But Gabe didn't think he'd be able to sleep that easily. He was too alert now, too aware of the sensual softness of her, the crush of her breasts against him, the teasing scent of her shampoo. The kisses they'd shared earlier came back to him in excruciating detail.

He fidgeted, restless and trying to get more comfortable as his arousal spiked to new levels.

"Mmm." Arianne burrowed closer, and he almost laughed. How could she feel so addictively good yet be torturing him at the same time?

The phone shrilled, and Arianne's eyes popped open, going wide as they met his. "Oh!"

He suspected that if there were enough light in the room he'd be watching her blush.

She started to roll away, but he hugged her first, just long enough to let her know he wasn't sorry she was there. When their gazes locked again, she no longer looked embarrassed at finding herself sprawled in such a position. Shadows fell across her features, but he could sense a new emotion in her. Dare he hope, desire?

He slid his hands from her back down to the curve of her butt. She moved against him, the friction overwhelming, even through his jeans.

"What about the phone?" she whispered, propping herself on one elbow.

The phone was the least of his problems. He wanted—needed—to kiss her again. But they weren't in Mistletoe town square now. They were alone in his bed. If they got carried away by the same passions they'd kindled in each other earlier, there was no question of how this would end. He would make love to Arianne Waide.

And then what? His conscience tried to make itself

heard over his libido. Gabe's only affairs in the past decade had been with women who either lived in neighboring towns or women who, like Nicole, wouldn't be in Mistletoe long. Arianne would probably be here for the rest of his life. What kind of bastard would seduce a woman like her, then leave without a backward glance? While Gabe thought Shane McIntyre was largely a horse's behind, the man had been accurate when he said Gabe wasn't worthy of her.

"Gabe?" His name was a husky caress on her lips.

"You were right," he said halfheartedly, dropping his hands to his sides. "I should get the ph—"

"It stopped ringing." She used his horizontal position to mitigate the difference in their height, moving up to nip at his neck and then his bottom lip.

His body tensed in piercing pleasure. "Arianne—"

"Kiss me," she said against his mouth.

God, yes. "Wait, I—"

She froze. "I'm so selfish! I'm hurting you, aren't I? Is your vision still blurred?"

How could he tell? He was nearly cross-eyed with lust anyway.

"You aren't hurting me." At least not in the way she meant. "But you don't know me well enough to do this."

"Shouldn't *I* get to decide that?" She poked him lightly in the chest.

"Not if you don't have all the facts," he countered.

Shushing his protests, she pressed two fingers against his mouth, then drew them down so that her index finger slipped between his lips. He sucked on the tip, reveling in the way her breathing sped up. Arianne was never shy about expressing herself. Making love to her would be—

"I know enough," she pledged, swiveling her hips so that she was astride him. "And I want you."

He surprised a gasp out of her when he pushed himself upright, gathering her to him for a searing, open-mouthed kiss that burned away the last of his qualms. Plunging his fingers through her hair, he slanted his mouth over hers. The clip she'd been wearing clattered to the hardwood floor and long blond waves fell forward, curtaining them.

Arianne burned with need. No one had ever kissed her like this. She felt dangerously, exhilaratingly out of control. She was greedy for more, wanted to explore the hollows and planes of his hard body. She started to pull back so that she could remove his T-shirt, and gasped when the motion rocked her against him, the sensation so exquisite that she rolled her hips a second time with slow deliberation.

He swore softly, then grabbed her waist, hauling her to him and kissing her breathless. Somehow he managed to unbutton the top half of her long shirt using only one hand, shoving the material backward so that it dropped away from her body. The cool air was a sensual balm against her overheated skin. Under the lacy cups of her bra, her nipples beaded into tight points.

She was unprepared for Gabe to roll them over suddenly, pinning her beneath him. Should a man with a head injury be moving so qui—? *Oh!* She inhaled sharply as he kissed her through the lace. The pleasure was nearly unbearable—she couldn't tell if she wanted him to keep going or if she needed a second to catch her breath.

Almost as if reading her mind, he gave her a moment's respite, stopping just long enough to pull his shirt over his head. *Wow.* Even in the darkened room, she could appreciate how his well-muscled arms tapered to a movie-screen-worthy chest and a stomach indented with a straight line down the middle, ringed with the faint outline of abs. Next to that kind of physical perfection, Arianne should probably feel self-conscious about how rarely she exercised, but instead the only feeling she experienced was giddiness at the thought of being able to touch him.

She trailed her fingers over the flat dip of his navel, toward the waistband of his jeans. Her fingers shook as she undid the button and the zipper. Gabe held himself as still as a predatory cat right before it pounced.

When she rubbed him through the cotton of the boxer-briefs, his head fell back, his expression strained and indefinably erotic. "Arianne."

He said her name like a pagan prayer. He made a pilgrimage of her body, worshipping with his hands and his lips. Her denim capris and then her bra vanished beneath his expert touch. By the time he slid a finger over the satiny material between her thighs, she was practically writhing with need. When he opened the nightstand drawer to get a condom, she almost sobbed with relief, long past ready to take him inside her.

She stroked him one last time, guided him to her center, her body bucking upward when he thrust into her. He braced himself above her, his muscles rigid with exertion as he watched her. She met his gaze as long as she could, until the intensity became too much, and she had to look away as the tremors built inside her. She closed her eyes, spasmed around him and let go, the ripples escalating into shock waves. Gabe finished with a wordless shout, then rolled flat onto his back, reaching for her hand among the tangled sheets and blanket. They lay there panting with their fingers entwined.

When Arianne noticed that he was pressing his temple with his free hand, she experienced a twinge of contrition. "Are you all right?"

"I could use some more of those pills," he admitted. "Other than that, I'm perfect."

Yes, you were. "I'll be right back," she said, shrugging into the shirt she'd worn earlier. She padded down the hall to the kitchen where she scooped the acetaminophen off the counter and poured a glass of water for Gabe. Standing in front of the refrigerator, she realized that she was famished.

"Thank you," Gabe told her when she returned. He'd flipped on the nightstand lamp, the soft golden glow bathing his skin.

She dropped the pills in his palm. "It's the least I can do." What had she been thinking, attacking a concussed guy? This probably had not been what the doctor had in mind when he'd instructed her to wake Gabe every few hours and check for a response.

"I only hope I didn't do you irreparable harm," she said ruefully.

A smile flirted around the corners of his mouth. "If you did, I forgive you. It was worth it."

She sat next to him, tucking her feet under her. "Any chance you're hungry? We never did have lunch, and I'm pretty sure we missed dinner, too."

He paused, as if taking stock. "Earlier I was nauseous, but now that you mention it, I'm starving."

"I could make us dinner," she volunteered, the offer making her incongruously bashful. The man had just seen her naked, but there was a different kind of intimacy in fixing him a meal in his home. It just felt so uncharacteristically domestic. "Although I should warn you, I'm not a very accomplished chef. My mother, bless her heart, tried to teach me, but I always wanted to be playing basketball out on the driveway or riding bikes with my brothers."

"Arianne, right now, you could serve me a burned grilled cheese sandwich made with stale bread, and I'd still think you were a goddess. The problem is I doubt I have much in the way of groceries. I stock up on the weekend and had planned to go later today."

She considered this, too hungry to get dressed and drive into town in search of sustenance. "Well, there's ice cream."

"Ice cream for dinner?" Gabe grinned at her. "Woman after my own heart."

IT WAS A SIX COURSE MEAL, if one counted chocolate syrup, sliced bananas and ice-cream flavors as courses. Dress was informal, Arianne only in a shirt and Gabe in formfitting boxer-briefs. They each picked out two varieties from the assortment in his freezer—Arianne had been curious about one called Hawaiian Vacation that included coconut slivers and macadamia nuts— and made large, sloppy sundaes.

Gabe didn't actually have a kitchen table, explaining that he mostly ate at the breakfast bar. But they opted not to perch on the high-backed stools and instead sat together on the navy plaid couch. Arianne, curious about everything from his choice of decorative touches to what movies he might have in his DVD collection, tried to take in her surroundings without seeming too nosy. It was a nice place, nothing fancy or fussy, but he used colors she thought worked well and he obviously wasn't a slob. Frankly, if the tables had been turned and she'd ended up with him as unexpected company this afternoon, she wasn't sure her place would have been as neat. It seemed like she was frequently on her way somewhere—to work, to her parents', out with friends— and she had a tendency to dump stuff in the chair closest to the door as she passed.

A picture in a wooden frame, sitting on top of the shelves of the entertainment center, caught her eye. It looked like a personal shot rather than a professionally taken photo, and a pretty young woman on a railed front porch was smiling at the camera. Judging by her clothes and hairstyle, the picture was at least a couple of decades old.

"Your mom?" Arianne hazarded a guess.

Gabe paused with his spoon in midair. "Yeah."

"Were you close?"

"No. She died before I was two weeks old. If it weren't for pictures, I wouldn't even know what she looked like." He said the words blandly, with no emotion, and she wondered how he really felt. Did it bother him that he'd been denied the chance to bond with her, or had he made his peace with that years ago, not truly missing something he'd never known?

"What happened?" she asked, wanting to know more about this man and the upbringing that had shaped him.

"Postsurgery complications. I was a really large baby and they decided to do a C-section." Again said eerily without inflection. Not sorrow or misplaced guilt that the C-section might have been his fault, simply a rote statement of fact. "She got an infection afterward, which is always dangerous, but she was diabetic, which made it harder to fight."

Thinking of how important her mother, Susan, had been to her all her life, Arianne got a lump in her throat. But nothing in Gabe's demeanor suggested he wanted to discuss his own feelings, so she found another outlet for her sympathy. "That must have been hard on your father."

Gabe's laugh was harsh. "And he never let me forget that. You should have seen his face when I, in the third grade, foolishly asked if there was a chance he might remarry, if I would ever have…" He trailed off, staring into space with such anger and pain that she couldn't believe she'd thought him emotionless moments before.

Had she done it again, pushed too hard?

No, she told herself. Even if Gabe didn't want to

admit it to himself, this was probably something he needed to deal with. Was this strain why he and his father weren't close? If Gabe was going to leave Mistletoe—her heart ached at the thought—then this might be his last chance to make peace with his dad. Although the past couldn't be altered, perhaps they could at least gain closure.

Relationships, familial or romantic, were messy, often painful, but extraordinarily worth the effort. Maybe Gabe just hadn't had anyone in his life to demonstrate how rewarding they could be. Arianne had taken a front-row look at her parents' long marriage and her brothers' relationships. David and Rachel had struggled for several years with infertility and one miscarriage before beautiful Bailey had been born, and Arianne had watched them cope with the stress on their marriage. It took special people to weather the bad times together instead of distancing themselves from the problems and from each other.

Sometimes you just needed help bridging the distance.

Gabe stood suddenly, his unfinished ice cream melting into a tricolor mess. "If you don't mind, I think I'm going to grab a shower."

She tried not to feel wounded by his abruptness. The man had been working outside all morning, been at the hospital this afternoon and had given her the best sex of her life less than an hour ago. He deserved the comfort of a hot shower. But she couldn't ignore the sense that he was once again retreating. Getting to her feet, she took the bowl from his hand.

"You go ahead," she told him. "I'll clean up out here."

"Thanks." His gaze lingered, softened for just a moment, but then he disappeared down the hall without another word. Soon she heard the pipes creak to life behind the walls as the water started. Trying not to fantasize about what it would have been like if Gabe had invited her to join him in the shower, she carried the bowls to the kitchen and rinsed them out.

She had just turned off the sink when she realized that his phone was ringing. *Nicole, again?* She tried not to feel cranky about that possibility.

But it was a different female voice that came through the answering machine. "Gabriel? This is Mindy Nelson. I probably shouldn't have called—you might be sleeping. But I was just so worried when I heard—"

Arianne decided that Gabe wouldn't mind her fielding this one. "Hello? Mrs. Nelson? This is Arianne Waide."

"Oh, hi, Arianne." Mindy sounded confused but pleased that someone had answered. "Are you at Gabe's house?"

"Yes, ma'am. I was with him this afternoon when he got hit on the head and drove him to the E.R."

"I heard all about it. Fawne Harris makes it sound as if he appeared out of nowhere and saved her son's life."

"Well, he did catch Ben and keep him from injury," Arianne admitted proudly.

She'd thought Gabe was a hero long before then— when he'd volunteered to help despite not having kids at Whiteberry and not being sure he wanted to, when he'd stood up to Shane on her behalf and when he'd offered today to manufacture a way to keep Ben and Toby out of trouble. If only they'd realized sooner how necessary that would be!

Mindy clucked her tongue. "What a blessing that Gabe was there—I think Fawne's ordering him roses. I heard about it at dinner tonight and got concerned about Gabe. I almost didn't call, what with it being after nine by the time I got home, but…well, I was afraid he didn't have anyone else to check in on him."

Arianne ached, wondering how many good and bad moments he *hadn't* been able to share with someone. "No need to worry, ma'am. I'm here."

"I'm glad. He's such a good man. Do you know, when he was building the deck for my yard, I was trying to teach my oldest how to drive so that he could get his license? We were struggling with the parallel parking, making each other tense, and Gabe took it over for me one afternoon. My son passed his test the following week."

"Gabe volunteered to teach your kid to parallel park? Gabriel Sloan?"

"I told you, he's a good guy. Speaking of which, will you let him know that I spoke to my brother-in-law? I really talked up Gabe, so if he wants to call and ask about job opportunities, the way has been paved."

Arianne scowled. Yet another woman was trying to help Gabe get out of Mistletoe. Why wasn't anyone trying to help him *stay?* "I'll pass that message along."

Once they hung up, Arianne realized that it had been hours since she'd looked at her phone. She probably should have checked in with Lilah and Tanner long ago.

Sure enough, when she retrieved her cell from her purse, she saw that she had three voice mail messages, all from Lilah's number.

Instead of taking the time to listen to them, she called her sister-in-law.

"There you are!" Lilah sounded equal parts exasperated and excited. "I've been trying to reach you. How's Gabe?"

"Doctor said it was a concussion. He seems all right now, slept for hours. He took some more acetaminophen and is in the shower. I'm supposed to stay so that there's someone to monitor him until tomorrow."

Lilah was silent.

"What?" Arianne asked defensively.

"Nothing. I was just thinking about you needing to stay the night. With Gabriel Sloan."

"Don't say it like that. It's so I can wake him up periodically, check his pupil size, make sure he's not throwing up. That kind of thing," Arianne said, trying for virtuous.

"Uh-huh. Well, if you're not comfortable staying out there, I can send Tanner over. He could sleep on the couch. He can sleep anywhere. Just ask him about the one-and-only time we saw a ballet together."

For all Arianne knew, *she'd* be bunking on the sofa. Judging by his tension when he'd left the room, Gabe was no longer under the thrall of what they'd shared earlier.

"I'm good here," she said. "But could you pick me up in the morning? My car's still at the festival site."

"Actually, Tanner moved it with our spare key just a

little while ago. That's one of the reasons I was trying to get in touch with you, to let you know it's at our house."

Arianne laughed. "Because it wasn't safe overnight in downtown Mistletoe?"

"I *know,*" Lilah agreed, a teasing lilt in her voice. "Talk to your brother. I guess he lived in the city too long. Call us in the morning when you're ready to go."

Arianne promised that she would and ignored the cheerful innuendo in her sister-in-law's voice when she advised Arianne to have a good night. They disconnected, and Arianne paused for a moment, listening. Gabe was still in the shower. Since she had nothing to do, she decided to go ahead and give free rein to her curiosity.

There was nothing of major interest to see in the kitchen, so she returned to the living room, scrutinizing the entertainment center. As far as she could tell, it was the only TV in the house, a nice, large flat-screen. She grinned when she noticed that he owned a video game system, although she only saw one controller.

Against the far wall of the converted barn was the old loft. A set of painted wooden stairs with no railing led up to a carpeted, only partially enclosed loft with a skylight in the slanted roof. He'd made it a library of sorts. His computer sat on a desk in the corner, but the rest of the narrow space was eaten up by a large bookshelf. The man either loved to read or a hundred books had been included in the purchase when he bought this place. His tastes were varied, from lots of nonfiction and do-it-yourself books to Zane Grey's Westerns, some of which were yellowed with age, to futuristic cop stories by J. D. Robb to a collection of comic essays by Dave Barry.

Suddenly the water switched off, and Arianne scrambled down the staircase, not wanting to look like the snoop she was. By the time Gabe reappeared—shirtless in a pair of low-slung running pants—she was resituated on the couch.

She cleared her throat, trying to break her gaze away from his chest. "I was thinking about it and, if you'd rather, I can sleep on the sofa. If that would make you more comfortable," she offered, but she—or someone else of his choosing—was staying the night. That part was nonnegotiable.

"Don't be silly." He frowned at her. "The couch's not half as comfortable as the bed. If you don't mind my snoring, you're welcome to share. I can keep my hands to myself."

That hadn't been what she was hinting at, but it probably was better for his recovery if she didn't jump him again tonight.

"I pulled out a towel for you," he said. "It occurred to me after I was already in that a good host probably would have let you shower first."

"That's all right. I wanted to wash the dishes and call Lilah anyway, let her know you're okay. And Mindy Nelson called to check on you."

"She did?"

Arianne nodded. "She heard about the injury and was worried."

He looked bemused by this.

"She also wants you to know that she put in a good word with her brother-in-law."

"Already?" He pressed his palms together, speaking almost to himself. "It's really happening. I set it in motion, and I'm really doing this."

Yep, he was really leaving Mistletoe. *Ya-freaking-hoo.*

"Gabe," she began, "I'm not sure I understand why you're going."

"What's there to understand?" He blinked at her. "You're the one who asked me why I'd stayed this long in the first place. Remember?"

"Yeah, but… That's just my point! Since you *have* stayed in Mistletoe so many years, why give up on us and leave now?"

"I'm not 'giving up.' I'm moving on. Moving *forward.*" His tone had chilled, and he was looking at her reprovingly. "You're such a proactive person, I thought you'd understand."

"No, I do. I understand," she said quietly. *But I want you to stay.*

Chapter Eleven

"Gabe?"

It had been so long since either of them spoke that the word sounded unnaturally loud in the dark room, but she knew he wasn't asleep. He hadn't fallen into that steady, deep breathing. Plus, even though the only contact between their carefully spaced bodies was the curve of his hand over her hip, she could feel the tension radiating through him.

"Yeah?"

"Earlier, before…I seduced you—"

"You seduced me?"

"Absolutely. The trick was making it seem like your idea."

"Well, excellent job." He sounded genuinely amused, relaxing slightly behind her. "Because I've been having that idea for days now."

She smiled against her pillow. *Me, too.* "You said that there were facts I didn't know about you. What were you going to tell me if I hadn't persevered?"

"You can't have it both ways, Ms. Waide," he repri-
manded. "It was a onetime offer, and you chose to skip
the conversation in favor of sex. You don't get the conversation now."

"Oh." She was silent a moment. "Did you get a
chance to check your messages while I was in the
shower? It seemed like the phone rang quite a bit this
afternoon."

He groaned. "If I'd known you were going to be this
chatty, I would have accepted your offer to bunk on
the couch."

"Sorry. Guess I'm having trouble falling asleep since
I don't usually take long naps in the late afternoon. Am
I keeping you awake?"

"Not really," he admitted. "I'm not used to sleeping
the evening away, either. Yeah, I checked messages. Another possible job lead from a friend and a couple of potential clients wanting to talk to me about installing
windows and an automatic garage door."

"I really admire self-employed entrepreneurs like you
and Brenna Pierce and Chloe Malcolm," she said. "I
work hard at the store, but it was there from the time I
was born. I can't imagine creating it from the ground up."

He snorted. "You could have your own shopping
mall up and running in time for the Christmas rush if
you put your mind to it."

She didn't respond to the exaggeration, but was
secretly pleased that he thought her so capable. "Still,
you guys are dependent on word of mouth and keeping
clients happy. I've got myself in trouble once or twice

by speaking my mind with a customer, but at least they can balance my bad day against the reputation of three generations of Waides."

"It's true your family is well respected," he said flatly.

She took the plunge. "You may not realize this, but Tara Hunaker has actually spread some rumors that could hurt your professional standing. She's suggested that she hired you to refinish her basement and the job didn't get done."

"That's one hundred percent true."

Arianne whipped her head around on the pillow, trying to read his expression in the dark. "It is?"

"Yes. Turned out Tara wasn't in the market for a carpenter but a gigolo. I explained the difference to her—using small words—and quit."

Arianne felt her smile stretch from ear to ear. "You did?" Oh, how she would have loved to have been a fly on the wall for *that* conversation.

"I did. With the exception of one short-term customer who doesn't actually live here, I don't get involved with the women who hire me. I learned my lesson early."

"Because of Shay Templeton?" The words tumbled out of their own volition and she held her breath, waiting to see if he lashed out at her for her presumption. Or, worse, ignored the question altogether.

"Because of Shay." He rolled from his side to his back, putting more space between them.

She didn't chase after him but waited patiently to see if he would confide in her.

"I was sixteen. She was my first lover. She'd told me

for weeks how cold her husband was, how he made her feel unwanted, unloved."

In addition to being a teenage boy brimming with hormones, Gabe had also been someone who could relate to being trapped in a home lacking in affection. Shay had played him well. It was likely she'd also been legitimately attracted to him, but that in no way excused an adult—a *married* adult, no less!—preying on a sixteen-year-old.

"I told her afterward that I loved her." His brittle chuckle dripped self-loathing. "Can you imagine anyone that naive? A single afternoon in her bed and I was vowing to take her away from Mistletoe. She laughed, told me I was a sweet kid, not bad for a virgin, but that she had no intention of giving up her house and husband. She was still trying to kick me out when he came home."

Arianne squirmed inwardly, wishing she hadn't opened this particular can of worms. It was hard to hear him reliving the raw pain inflicted by the lover who'd calculated a premeditated seduction, then callously dismissed him.

"I shouldn't have left," he said hoarsely. "I saw how furious Templeton was, I should have stayed to protect her. But she wanted me to go, and I…"

He'd been hurt and confused and humiliated. Arianne was sorry for the senseless deaths, but she was angry with the long-dead Shay Templeton, not only for creating the tragedy but for embroiling a sixteen-year-old kid in the middle of it and permanently robbing him of his innocence.

"Thank you for telling me this," she whispered. "The fact that you can even discuss it is a good sign. It means—"

"All it means is that I don't want you to have any illusions about me," he snapped. "I slept with another man's wife and slunk off like a coward when their fight turned volatile. That's who I am. Maybe you were right when you accused me of 'giving up.' It certainly wouldn't be the first time I did that, but make no mistake, I'm leaving Mistletoe."

She bit the inside of her cheek, fighting her natural inclination to argue, to tell him that she didn't have illusions, that she saw him more clearly than he saw himself. She saw the past hurts and the honorable man he'd grown into despite them. She saw someone who had retreated into solitude, working alone, living alone, playing video games alone.

I don't want you to have any illusions about me. He was trying to give her all the reasons why he was the wrong man for her, too much of a risk to be entrusted with her heart. A week ago, she would have agreed. Now she thought it was more complicated than that.

Hadn't she been thinking only earlier tonight that the potential rewards of love were worth the struggle and effort? Rather than simply labeling him the wrong man, couldn't she instead help him become the right one?

WHEN ARIANNE WOKE on Sunday morning, she was alone in the bed. A note on the nightstand said that Gabe would be back in a few minutes. After a moment's deliberation over whether it was an invasion of personal space, she decided to pillage his closet for a shirt to wear. Hers was beyond grungy after twenty-four hours. She thumbed through a few hangers and laughed when she found a red T-shirt, faded and soft from many washings, that said Waide Supply above the pocket. Her dad had given them out as promotional items one year to every customer who spent more than sixty dollars in a visit. She had one in blue, but it didn't hang nearly to her knees the way Gabe's did.

Once she'd changed, she got a piece of sugar-free gum out of her purse in lieu of a toothbrush. She was securing her hair in a ponytail when she heard the front door close.

"Arianne?"

Just the sound of his voice thrilled her, but she tried not to sound like a squealing girl with a crush. "Back here."

He appeared in the bedroom doorway holding a white sack with the Dixieland Diner logo on it. "Mornin'. I thought you might like something besides ice cream for breakfast."

"That was thoughtful." Her stomach rumbled at the smell of sausages and…was that syrup she detected? "Did you get us pancakes?"

At his nod, she thought, *I adore you.*

Today, they decided in unspoken agreement to eat at the breakfast bar. The breakfast dishes were not going to balance in her lap as easily as the ice-cream bowl. She sat on one of the stools while he got silverware out of a drawer.

Tossing his cell phone on the counter, Gabe said offhandedly, "Oh, I called Lilah on my way back from the diner to let her know you'd be ready to go soon. She should be here in about twenty minutes. I figured you'd be in a hurry for a fresh change of clothes." His mouth quirked in a half grin, exposing his left dimple, as he took in the too-big shirt.

She smiled back as it was impossible to be annoyed with a man who bought you buttermilk pancakes with turkey sausage and fresh fruit. But she would have called Lilah herself. Was he trying to get rid of her?

He sat next to her and they ate in silence. Arianne racked her brain for the best way to handle the situation. She'd had a few lovers in her life, but they'd been steady boyfriends, guys she'd known well and had been in relationships with long before they found their way to her bed. Did Gabe consider last night a onetime event? The thought was bleak. But since she'd assured him she knew all she needed to take the leap, she could hardly press him now for answers and commitments.

As far as Arianne was concerned, they had a future of some sort. One of them just didn't know it yet. Rather than informing him of her own feelings and encouraging him to consider his, she decided to exercise rarely used tact. They would talk later. For now, he was still finishing his breakfast and Lilah's car was coming up the long driveway.

Arianne glanced out the window. "That's my ride."

Gabe opened the door and Lilah walked inside looking like an old-fashioned suitor come a-courtin'. She held a bouquet, a picture of some sort and a shoe box with a bow on it.

"What's all this?" Gabe asked, staring at the roses as if they were live grenades on stems.

"These—" Lilah handed over the flowers "—are from Fawne as a thank-you. There's a note. This is something Ben drew for you. And Quinn got you this very manly first-aid kit as her way of saying she hopes you feel better soon."

He set the box on the bar to open it, and Arianne laughed at the sight of a green-and-brown camouflage-print ice pack and a box of adhesive bandages printed with monster trucks. He barely looked at her, instead staring at the odd assortment of gifts in disbelief.

"Seems like an awful lot of fuss," he said.

Lilah raised an eyebrow. "Well, Ben's awful important to his friends and family. We hate to think what would have happened to him if you hadn't been there. By the way, Jack Allen has apologized a dozen times for just leaving that ladder propped like that and not giving anyone a heads-up that it was there. He loaded it onto Nick Zeth's truck, along with the bouncy balls. They're planning to bring it by today and help with the pirate ship construction if you need it."

Even though Gabe shifted uncomfortably at this announcement, Arianne couldn't be more delighted by the news. *This* was the Mistletoe she knew and loved—neighbors and friends helping each other out and banding together. It was high time Gabe got to be a part of that Mistletoe, too. She just hoped it wasn't too late.

Lilah fished her keys out of her pocket. "You about ready, Ari?"

Translation, was Arianne prepared for the interrogation that was going to take place the second the two women were alone in the car? She decided that she wasn't going to confide in Lilah, not yet. Gabe was such a private person that telling Lilah any of what he'd shared would feel like a betrayal. And as far as their making love… For now, that was hers alone, inviolable and not open for discussion.

Arianne slid her purse strap onto her shoulder. "I'm good to go."

Gabe walked them to the door, making no move to touch her but smiling into her eyes when he said, "I'm sure I'll be talking to you soon."

"Count on it." And then, since Lilah had already seen them kissing anyway and Arianne had never been good at denying her impulses, she stretched up—relieved he met her halfway—and kissed him quickly across the lips.

Lilah didn't say anything until she'd started the car. "Tanner wanted to come pick you up, but I vetoed him. I figured you wouldn't want to deal with the whole macho, overprotective brother vibe and his giving Gabe the stink-eye."

"Good call."

"But don't be surprised when we have dinner with the family tonight. They're going to ask questions."

Arianne smirked, deducing that this oh-so-considerate warning was just a way of Lilah leading into her own inquiries. "Let 'em ask. I love my family, and it's perfectly normal for them to have an interest in my life. Of course, they'll also have to understand that I'm a grown woman who doesn't have to answer to anyone else."

Lilah snorted. "Yeah, try that with your brothers and dad and see how well it goes over."

Playing with the hem of her T-shirt, Arianne asked, "Do you think they'll like him? Dad and Dave and Tanner? It was different for you and Rachel coming into the family. Mom and I were thrilled not to be outnumbered anymore and we're not quite as...tribal as the guys. They close ranks sometimes without even meaning to."

Gabe had endured enough of that already. If Arianne was successful in winning him over, the Waides were going to welcome him into the clan with open arms, damn it.

"They just want what's best for you," Lilah said. "Same as you do for them. I can't promise they won't threaten to beat his ass if he ever hurts you, but if you're happy, they'll accept him. Does he make you happy?"

Arianne thought about the acrid tang of rejection she experienced whenever he found a reason to walk away from her. It wasn't promising that he'd had thirty years' practice in numbing himself to his emotions and almost no practice with healthy, loving relationships.

"Not yet." She bit her lip, looking out the window. "But he will."

Chapter Twelve

The next committee meeting for the festival was Tuesday night at town hall and would precede the monthly open town meeting that many of the volunteers were planning to attend anyway. When Arianne had called Gabe yesterday to check on how he was feeling, he'd told her that he probably wouldn't make it.

"I don't need to be there for the discussion," he'd said. "I'm just the hired muscle."

"Yes," she'd agreed solemnly. "We only want you for your pirate ship. And your booty."

He didn't immediately respond, but she heard the laugh he tried to smother. Then he explained that, with Nick's and Jack's help, actual construction of the pieces was done, but Gabe thought his time was better spent sanding and painting than sitting in the town hall.

Which suited her nefarious purposes just fine, she realized now as the mayor called the town meeting to order. An idea was beginning to take shape in her mind. The agenda was posted on the whiteboard behind the mayor's head and included some of their town's annual traditions, like the Winter Wonderland ball. And Mistletoe's Man of the Year, someone they voted for in early November and who was given the honor of leading the Thanksgiving parade.

With half an ear, Arianne listened to Pat Donavan talk about suggested changes to how the town's intramural sports were run, followed by Stanley Dean outlining the budget for a town beautification project and Belle Fulton's report from the chamber of commerce. Finally they moved to the next to last item: Mistletoe Man of the Year. Anticipation had Arianne fidgeting in her seat so much that Quinn shot her a quizzical look.

"As you all know, we took preliminary nominations for the Man of the Year at last month's meetings. Those included our new high school coach Dylan Echols—"

This elicited a loud, admiring whistle from Chloe Malcolm, Dylan's fiancée, and friendly laughter from everyone seated around her.

The mayor raised a brow. "May I continue? We also have local fireman Nick Zeth, two-time former Man of the Year, David Waide, and Petey Gruebner, nominated again this year by Petey Gruebner," the mayor concluded with an aggrieved sigh.

At this, Petey nudged his wife, who'd been busily knitting and not paying much attention to the proceedings. She clapped politely before returning to what looked like a scarf big enough to keep a giraffe's neck warm.

"At this time," the mayor said, "I'll open the floor for

any final nominations to consider before we vote at the November meeting in a few weeks."

Arianne shot to her feet. Next to her Quinn groaned, "She isn't."

Lilah laughed in the row behind them. "She *is!*"

"Mr. Mayor, I nominate Gabriel Sloan."

"Is that your idea of a joke, Ms. Waide?" An outraged masculine voice boomed from the back of the room.

Dreading what she was about to see, Arianne turned. Oh, God, she hadn't even considered this possibility when she'd devised her spontaneous plan thirty minutes earlier. Because she'd been here so early, she was seated close to the front and had been chatting with other people on the festival committee right up until the time the mayor had called order. Arianne hadn't seen Earline and Robert Ortz, Shay Templeton's parents, come in and take seats near the door.

Robert was on his feet, his face nearly purple beneath his snow-white hair. His wife, still seated, was squeezing his hand.

Whatever Arianne thought privately about Shay and the mistakes she'd made, she wouldn't wish losing a child on any parent. She tried to sound respectful even as she said firmly, "No, sir, I was serious."

"That boy was the reason my baby girl was killed!"

The "boy" had been a victim, too, albeit in a less dramatic and permanent way than Shay, and was now a man. "With all due apologies for your loss, that was fourteen years ago, and Gabe wasn't even in the house when it happened. None of us really knows what happened. How long should he be punished for a perceived crime?"

People were squirming and whispering, shooting sympathetic glances at the Ortz family, collectively uncomfortable with the direction the meeting had taken. Cici Hunaker was openly smirking, one primly dressed woman in the front row looked ready to hyperventilate. *Hell*. This hadn't been what Arianne had in mind at all. She'd wanted to talk about all the work Gabe had done for the town over the years; sure, a lot of it was his paid occupation, but that wasn't so very different from Nick Zeth, who was a salaried fireman. In the past five years Gabe had helped repair houses after some spring tornadoes had blown through, working twelve-hour days to help people get their lives back together as quickly as possible. He'd patched and improved and converted homes, all the while never truly seeing this town as his home.

He was good to the town's senior citizens, donated his time on behalf of the elementary children in this town, had even risked the high-stress potential of teaching a teen to drive. Arianne had wanted to refocus everyone on those qualities, not dredge up the ancient past. But she found herself tongue-tied in the glare of Robert Ortz, not wanting to say anything that sounded as if she were dismissing his loss.

The mayor banged his gavel on the podium. "Robert, why don't you take your seat?" he asked gently. "Can we get you anything? A glass of water? Earline? Now, Ms. Waide, continue with your nomination, but keep it short. We, er, have other business to discuss."

The only thing left on the agenda was the Winter Wonderland, annually held at the Mistletoe Inn, and Arianne knew that wasn't the real reason the mayor wanted her to wrap up with haste.

She took a deep breath and tried again. "I don't deny that Gabe may have made some mistakes in his past. I wager everyone in this room has made mistakes. But he's part of Mistletoe, quietly helping us when we need him."

"Hear, hear!" Fawne Harris said.

Arianne darted her a grateful glance. "I think the other nominees are wonderful men, but come on, my brother doesn't need the honor a *third* time. Do we really want to feed his ego?"

"Hey!" David called out with mock indignation.

A few people chuckled, helping dispel the earlier tension. Next to him, Rachel patted his knee and whispered loudly, "It's okay, honey, *I* still appreciate you."

Feeling braver now, Arianne continued her appeal. "And Dylan's a great guy—we're lucky that he decided to move back to town last spring—but Gabe's *been* here year after year to help us rebuild after storms. I heard a rumor that he wouldn't take any money from the church after he was hired to fix the leak in the sanctuary wall." If the townspeople were allowed to pass along the sordid Tara-generated gossip, why not the redeeming stuff, too? Reverend Billings, seated on the other side of the main aisle, nodded.

"I'm sure most of you have heard about the walk-the-plank attraction he's been building as a special fundraiser for the festival. And ask Mindy Nelson's son if he would have his driver's license without Gabe's help," Arianne added.

"I second the nomination," Dele Momsen said. She shot a compassionate look at the Ortzs, but her voice didn't waver when she lent her support.

"All right then," the mayor said. "Thank you, ladies, and thank you, Arianne, for making your case. His name has been officially entered for the vote. Any other nominations?"

When no one immediately said anything, the mayor moved rather desperately to the next topic.

Leaning so close their heads almost touched, Quinn whispered, "And what did Gabe have to say about this when you dutifully talked it over with him first?"

Arianne smiled weakly. "I'm hoping he likes surprises."

IT WAS A GOOD THING there was no one else in the store Wednesday evening because Gabe would have terrified any onlookers when he stormed in, demanding, "What the hell were you thinking?"

Déjà vu, but not.

Exactly two weeks ago tonight, Arianne had found herself alone in her father's store with Gabriel Sloan, just as they were now. Except two weeks ago, she'd had to dig deep just to get one-word responses from him. Now he was in here vocalizing entire sentences. Loudly.

"Good evening. Welcome to Waide Supply," she said brightly.

"Is this a joke to you?" he asked, stalking closer.

"No, but you bit my head off, and it left me temporarily unable to think of what to say, so I went with a classic." She stopped smiling. "I would love to talk to you, but I don't like being yelled at."

"And I don't like being a town punch line! Damn it, Arianne, I try to stay *out* of the limelight. It's one of the reasons I stopped going to On Tap. I got tired of deflecting verbal jabs from men and getting hit on by tipsy women dared by their friends." He raked a hand through his hair, looking slightly calmer now that he'd vented some of his frustration. "I heard about last night."

"I figured." Frankly it had taken longer than she'd expected for him to find out and track her down. She really should've told him herself, but she'd thought he might take the news better from a neutral third-party source.

Derision sparked in his gray eyes. "Were you trying to embarrass me?"

"That's not fair!" She recalled how her knees had knocked together when she'd made her public declaration, struggling to find appropriate words that would somehow characterize all that was good about Gabe yet wouldn't be inexcusably offensive to the Ortzs, objective words that wouldn't betray her own vested interest, that she was falling— "I spoke from the heart last night. Anyone who suggests that I did so lightly is an idiot! And a liar."

Gabe stood on the other side of the register counter, his head cocked as he examined her. "Are you about to cry?"

"What? Of course not." She widened her eyes, trying to keep from blinking, lest a tear break free. She hadn't realized she was getting so emotional about this.

"Ari." He reached out and swiped his index finger across her lashes. A teardrop glistened on the pad of his finger. "Don't. I'm not worth tears."

"You are! That was my point to the town. You don't even know your own worth, Gabe."

He closed his eyes, looking pained by her praise.

"It's true," she persisted obstinately. "I grew up with a strict but fair father who loves me and two big brothers, so I have high standards for men. I'm not just some silly girl easily swayed by great biceps. You have your own code of honor, you have this great, barely tapped reservoir of humor, you have heart." *Even if it's been broken for a long time.*

A muscle in his jaw twitched as he met her gaze, his expression enigmatic. Then he braced his hands on the counter and jumped, swinging his feet over and dropping down on her side.

Arianne's mouth went dry at the display of physical prowess and his sudden proximity to her. "Technically," she murmured, "nonemployees aren't allowed to be back here."

He cupped her shoulders and crushed his mouth against hers in a conflicted kiss. She knew he was still annoyed about the nomination, but that she'd moved him with what she'd said. Deliberately gentle, she kissed him back, sucking at his bottom lip, running her tongue over his. After a second, any anger in his gesture had been replaced with simple, slow pleasure.

Breaking their kiss, he pressed his brow to the top of her head. "You're a difficult woman to stay angry with."

"I'm sorry I made you angry," she said.

He chuckled. "But not sorry you nominated me in the first place?"

"Take the apology you can get," she advised. "I have a question for you."

Leaning against the counter, he folded his arms over his chest. "Is it 'Hey, Gabe, do you mind if I bring you up at tonight's town hall meeting?' because the time for *that* request would have been yesterday."

"If it makes you feel any better, I didn't know beforehand. It's not like it was something I've been secretly plotting for a week. I was looking at the meeting agenda and it suddenly came to me."

"You know, you're allowed to have impulses and not act on them."

She shot him a dubious look. "Did you *just* meet me?" Somehow she found the discretion not to point out that he'd been repressing his emotions and urges for years and that it had resulted in his mostly being isolated and grim. Did he even realize how much more he'd smiled and laughed in the past week?

"Go ahead and ask your question while I'm ready for it," he said. "Otherwise, you might spring it on me later at some unsuspecting moment."

Another layer to the déjà vu she'd experienced earlier; she was about to invite him on a date, as she had that Wednesday two weeks ago. But since he'd just been seducing her mouth with his, she thought her odds had improved substantially. "Be my date for the festival?"

"Your date?" He tried to take a step back but stumbled at the realization that he was already against the counter and had nowhere to go. "I…"

You're kidding me! She'd struck out *again?*

He brushed her long hair away from her face, his smile sad. "I've hurt your feelings."

"Tell me why you won't go with me. I mean, I'll be working part of the time, but only in shifts. The rest of the day I have to walk around, stuffing my face with really great food, letting a big strong guy try to win me teddy bears, that kind of thing."

"Look, I don't deny the attraction between us," he said. "I can barely be in the same room with you and keep my hands off you. I'm weak enough that, for whatever time I have left in Mistletoe, I do want to see you. But not…publicly."

Her jaw dropped. "So I'm all right to take to bed in the privacy of your own home as long as you don't have to be seen with me?"

"It's not like that! I'm not ashamed of you, I'm *thinking* of you. Tanner told me that you guys have known Shane McIntyre for years, but that friendship's rocky now. Because of me. And I didn't hear only about you nominating me yesterday. Beau Albright told me who was there, that you were teetering on the brink of scandal and harsh feelings. You've never been on the outside, and trust me, you don't want to be."

"It won't be like that," she said earnestly. "Just the opposite. I can help you! People like you—or they would if you gave them a chance."

"I'm not looking to make new friends here. I'm getting up at five in the morning to drive to Kennesaw tomorrow," he told her. "I have an interview. And I've faxed résumés to a small community college in South Carolina and a construction company in Florida."

His words battered her optimism, deflated the hope that he shared her feelings and might find the courage to build on them. She was gutsy, but she couldn't be brave enough for both of them.

"Good luck on the interview," she said woodenly. She sidestepped him, needing some physical outlet. Behind the counter was a rag and some glass cleaner. This seemed like as good a time as any to scrub the hell out of the front windows.

He hovered behind her, not saying anything, his mere presence ratcheting up the tension inside her until she wanted to scream, *Go away. Or hold me.* She couldn't decide which she yearned for more.

"I could use a friend," he finally said. She knew the admission cost him. "I'm not used to business interviews, and I'm…"

"Nervous?" she supplied, melting a little at this show of vulnerability.

"Can I call you when I get back? If you can spare a few hours in the evening, maybe we can have a late dinner together and I can tell you about it."

She shook her head. "You mean a dinner behind closed doors. Or, at best, an extremely platonic dinner in public that couldn't be construed as a date."

He glared, not pleased with the way she'd rejected his olive branch.

"I'm sorry, Gabe. You may have noticed I don't do half measures well." It wasn't that she was purposely trying to give him an ultimatum, only that she had to be true to herself and protect her heart as best she could this late in the game. Relationship sacrifices were worth it when the participants were *in* a relationship. He was only willing to skate by on the shadowed edges. "I'm an all-or-nothing gal."

"That you are." He looked away, taking several deep breaths, then reached for the door. "Goodbye, Arianne."

Chapter Thirteen

When Zachariah Waide came into the store after his dinner hour, Arianne didn't even try to pretend that she was all right.

"Dad, can I leave early tonight? Please?"

His brow creased with worry as he looked at her. "Is this about that young man?"

Even though her father had been working last night at the store instead of attending the town meeting, she was sure he'd heard all about it.

"Yeah." She swallowed, determined not to let tears well up again. "It is."

With a sigh, he hugged her to him. "Go home, call some of your girlfriends, listen to some maudlin music or whatever it is you kids do to cope these days. It will be all right. Look at your brothers—if both those yahoos could find lasting true love, you will, too."

She knew that her father adored her brothers and was only trying to make her laugh. He did get a watery little giggle out of her that made her feel one percent better. Now she just had to figure out what to do about the other ninety-nine.

Deciding that her dad had been on the right track, she climbed into her car, locked the doors and picked up her cell phone. She wanted to get in touch with Quinn before she started home since her friend lived in the opposite direction.

Quinn answered immediately. "Hello?"

"Thank goodness you're there! It's Ari." She sniffled. "I could use a sympathetic ear. You free tonight?"

"Umm. For you, I can be," Quinn said loyally. "I mean, Patrick and I were going to a movie, but—"

"Don't you dare cancel! I'll think of something."

"Hang on. Brenna's on the other line. She agreed to wait while I clicked over in case it was a telemarketer or something." Quinn left without getting a response but was back just as fast. "She's about to call you, okay?"

"Thanks, Quinn."

Brenna must have dialed the second she disconnected her phone call with Quinn. "Hey, Arianne, everything all right?"

"No. Are you sure *you* don't have plans tonight? I'm not trying to sabotage my friends' love lives."

"Adam's surgeries got behind today, and he'll be working late. I'm all yours. You want to meet at the diner?"

"Too public," Arianne heard herself say. It was an ironic answer since it sounded a lot like what Gabe had said to her. But after facing down people last night at town hall, she wanted to minimize the chance of who she might run into this evening.

"Okay. You want to come over and talk at my house? I have ice cream."

Her mind flashed to Gabe's fully stocked freezer, and she bit her lip. "I'm on my way. But I think I'm off ice cream for a while."

"Is IT WEIRD TO THINK I might be falling in love?" Arianne was tucked up onto a love seat, Brenna's cat purring comfortably in her lap. "I mean, I've known him my entire life—sort of—and then within two weeks, bam! Does that even make sense?"

Brenna set her bowl down on the coffee table with a shrug. "I'm not sure there's a one-size-fits-all timetable, but it didn't take me a full month to know I was in love with Adam."

For Arianne's brother David, it had been love at first sight. He claimed that he'd known the day he met Rachel that he wanted to marry her, but he'd waited to share that information with her so she wouldn't think he was crazy. Tanner had been a different story altogether. It had taken him years—not to mention losing Lilah and later having to win her back—to figure out they should be together for the rest of their lives.

"I can't actually be in love." Arianne glowered. "I'm not really that self-destructive, am I? I've dated some nice guys, some cute guys, but there wasn't that… connection. And now I fall for the worst possible man?" There'd never been anyone truly special she'd wanted to go to the Winter Wonderland dance with. Now there was, but he was hoping to be gone from town by then.

Brenna tilted her head, regarding her curiously. "After everything you said in town hall about his good qualities, why would you call him the worst possible man?"

"Because he wants nothing to do with Mistletoe or the people of Mistletoe," Arianne said glumly.

"Oh. That might make his being Mistletoe's Man of the Year a bit awkward."

"You think?" Arianne sighed. "I know, I know, I should have thought the nomination through better." She'd been trying to help, to show the town a different side of him, to show Gabe he could belong here.

"Look at this as a hiccup," Brenna consoled her. "There was a time when I thought Adam and I didn't stand a chance."

"But that was because of geography and working out the complications with his children. There was no question that he *wanted* to be with you."

"You don't think Gabe wants to be with you?"

"Only under the cover of darkest night," she said sarcastically. "He doesn't want people to think we're dating because he's afraid it might hurt my reputation or something. And I don't think he wants me to get too attached because he's leaving." The latter might actually be a valid point, except she was pretty sure the damage had already been done.

"He's trying to protect you. That's sweet." At Arianne's scowl, Brenna quickly added, "Misguided and outdated, but sweet. Maybe he just doesn't know how tough you are."

Arianne absently scratched the cat under her chin. "I don't feel very tough."

Brenna laughed. "You must not remember the advice you gave me when I was lovelorn. Quinn made some comment about loving and letting go and you were offended that women might be expected to just graciously let go. I believe you suggested that I should 'track his butt down.'"

"That's ridiculous," Arianne scoffed, "and proof that people probably shouldn't take advice from me. I mean, sure it sounds bold and proactive, but I can't just club Gabe over the head and... Wait, *can* I club him over the head?"

Brenna smiled. "You might revisit talking to him first."

Why not? Considering the depth of her feelings for him, wasn't it worth another stab at conversation? It wasn't as if she had anything to lose. She could give them both a few days to think, then call him after the festival. Maybe she'd be pleasantly surprised by the results.

And as for knocking him upside the head? Well, it never hurt to have a Plan B.

"Looks good, man." Nick Zeth smiled in approval. The festival was due to open its figurative doors in forty minutes, and the pirate plank was ready to go. Dele Momsen had even purchased some spongy foam swords for the youngsters to brandish...and an eye patch for Gabe that he'd put in his back pocket and was trying to forget about.

"I appreciate your help with it this week," Gabe told the other man.

Nick and Shane McIntyre had played high school baseball together and been friends in all the years since. So considering Shane's animosity toward Gabe, Nick's easygoing assistance and jovial attitude had come as a pleasant surprise. Maybe Gabe had been too quick to make assumptions about people.

"Don't mention it. I had fun," Nick said. Then he adopted a mock glare. "Even if I was helping 'the competition.' I hear you're the one to beat for Mistletoe Man of the Year."

"More like the long shot, but if by some chance I did win, you're welcome to take my spot on the parade float."

Nick laughed. "Hey, I don't need your pity. If you win, I'll start mounting my campaign for next year early. If you don't need any more help, I'm off to stake a place in line."

Gabe looked around. None of the attractions were open yet. "Which line is that?"

Nick jerked his thumb toward the library. The streets had been closed to vehicular traffic for the day, and around the corner from where they stood, in front of the building, were myriad stalls and games. "Kissing booth, dude. Somehow they talked Candy Beemis into donating half an hour of her precious time, but later in the day it will be Holly Devereaux, oo la la, and Arianne."

"Arianne *Waide?*" How had he not known about this? The woman he wanted to kiss every time he saw her had neglected to mention that she'd be selling her kisses to anyone who walked by. Jealousy flared inside him, and he was glad Nick left before glimpsing his dark expression.

It's for a good cause, he told himself. When that failed to lower his blood pressure, he reminded himself that it was none of his business whom Arianne bestowed her kisses on. Hadn't he walked out of her life three nights ago? She certainly hadn't made any attempt to contact him since, which was telling.

I miss her. He squelched the thought. Breaking off contact was for the best. If he felt her absence after only three days, what would it be like if he kept seeing her and then moved away? The Kennesaw job, which he knew he wouldn't be getting, had actually been his strongest lead in Georgia.

"I like you, Mr. Sloan," the interviewer had told him. "But the truth is, I've seen three other applicants who already *have* experience on all the machines we use. We also function as a pretty tight crew. You work alone on most of your jobs?"

Alone. *Yep, that about sums me up.* In the end Gabe had thanked the man for his time and got back in his truck, not sure if he was relieved, disappointed or both. He'd never thought he would be glad to see the Welcome to Mistletoe sign.

Then again, he'd never been driving back toward Arianne.

"Mr. Sloan?"

Gabe turned to find the mayor offering a handshake.

The other man nodded toward the partial ship deck. "Have we given this thing a test run into the pit yet?"

"Yes, sir. Nick Zeth and a couple of his firefighter buddies were knocking each other in, and everything held up just fine. But I plan to stay close today and keep an eye on it. Safety first, right?"

"That's the spirit! And thanks again for putting this together. It's never easy to ask constituents for money, especially in these economic times, so if we're going to take donations from them, I'm glad we found a way to make it fun. Speaking for the citizens of Mistletoe, we appreciate your help."

Gabe almost strangled on a disbelieving laugh. Fourteen years ago, he'd expected to be run out of town on a rail—with his father leading the charge—and now the *mayor* was thanking him for his efforts on behalf of the town?

"I'm sure I'll be seeing you later," the mayor said. "I suspect I'll be taking the plunge multiple times today. Probably with my wife holding the other end of the sword."

Festival-goers were beginning to descend on town square; the noise level was increasing exponentially. People calling greetings to each other, volunteers testing out the sound systems in the bingo tent and at the gazebo, kids crying and laughing. And somewhere close by, a man letting out a wolf whistle.

He thought he recognized Nick's voice hollering appreciatively, "Helloooo, saucy wench."

A woman's laugh. *Arianne.*

"That's *Captain* Saucy, Pirate Queen, you scurvy knave." She sounded lighthearted and sexy.

It was frankly a bit depressing to learn that while he'd been standing here thinking about how much he missed her after such a short time, second-guessing how he'd left things the other night, her mood hadn't been dampened one bit. Then again, Arianne had always been irrepressible. It was one of the things he loved about her. In a manner of speaking.

He rested one hand at the pocket of his jeans and strolled casually forward. Did he look convincingly like someone just scoping out the lay of the land, or was it obvious he was a poor sap pining for the sight of a beautiful woman and onetime lover?

As he rounded the corner of the library, he nearly collided with Arianne, which meant *she'd* been coming to see *him*. He smiled, feeling happier than he had all week.

"Hey, sorry about that," he said. "I just— *What are you wearing?*"

"My swashbuckling pirate garb." She cocked her hip, beaming at him. "You like?"

Chapter Fourteen

Too bad Gabe had only a false veneer of a ship and not the real thing. He wanted nothing more than to toss Arianne over his shoulder and take her to his bunk to have his wicked way with her.

Gold hoop earrings peeked out through her long blond hair, which was loose and flowing beneath a jaunty brown tricorn. Although the dark corset-style leather vest she wore stopped short of being inappropriately risqué, it did enhance her cleavage enough that he couldn't stop remembering how she looked beneath her clothes. She had on a ruffled, off-the-shoulder long-sleeved cranberry shirt that hung down just low enough to cover her butt. Her dark brown leggings fit like a second skin, and he found himself fascinated by the thigh-high boots that somehow made her petite legs look a mile long.

At her hip hung a plastic cutlass, but he could have told her she didn't need a weapon. One look at her and men would line up to surrender.

"Holly said she'd dress up for the booth, too," Arianne told him, "but apparently our definitions of costume aren't quite the same. She's wearing a sundress with a bandanna around her neck, a black-and-white hat with the skull and crossbones on it and a parrot broach on her shoulder. Think I went overboard?"

"Isn't that the theme of the day?" He managed a tight smile, still trying to get his desire under control enough to speak intelligently.

"Usually I pull out all the stops for Halloween, but I may not be dressing up this year, so today's my one big hurrah."

"You look…wow."

"Thank you." She ducked her head, and he realized that she seemed more timid today than he'd first realized. Was that why she'd been speaking so quickly—not babbling exactly, but not calm, either? She swallowed. "I was on my way to find you."

"Yeah?" He must be the luckiest man in a hundred-block radius to have a woman like this seek him out.

"I wanted to know about your interview." She shifted her weight, meeting his gaze, composed again. Had he imagined her flash of nerves? "How'd it go?"

"I didn't get the job."

"Oh. I'm sorry to hear that."

Was she? Would he want her to be?

"Gabe." She caught her bottom lip between her teeth. "Are you busy after this? I was hoping maybe we could talk."

"No—I mean, yes. No to the first question," he backpedaled. Would they be able to reach some kind of compromise, instead of ending on Wednesday's disastrous note? "After this, I'm all yours."

GABE HADN'T PARTICIPATED in one of the town's festivals since he was a boy, but even as distracted as he was today by thoughts of Arianne, he was enjoying himself. As predicted, the mayor and his wife put on quite a spectacle for the crowd when she forced him to "walk the plank." A few of the Whiteberry faculty members chipped in to have Patrick thrown into "Davy Jones's locker," as a kind of initiation.

Patrick grumbled teasingly from within the ball pit, "Whatever happened to the days when folks said howdy by baking the new guy a cake?"

Lilah Waide also got tagged three different times by her students to go off the plank into the pit; by the third time, though, she'd caught a grinning Tanner actually giving the kids dollar bills.

"There will be payback," she cheerfully threatened her husband as Gabe helped her out of the pit.

Quinn passed by midmorning to check in on the festivities and to rather thoughtfully bring Gabe a freshly made funnel cake—also known as an elephant ear because of its size and shape. Warm and gooey with powdered sugar, the fried dough dessert was almost too big for one person to eat alone, and he caught himself scanning the crowd for Arianne. Even though he knew that she was busy elsewhere, he automatically wanted to share this with her, see her smile at the first sweet bite.

He wanted to kiss away the dots of sugar she'd no doubt have clinging to the corner of her lips.

The thought reminded him that she was working in the kissing booth. Now that he'd seen her attire for the day, the jealousy he'd battled earlier returned to gnaw at him.

"How are things going over at Arianne's booth?" he asked Quinn, hoping he sounded nonchalant rather than covetous.

The look she gave him was far too knowing. "Have you seen the poster over there? It's a big set of lips that represents how much money they're trying to raise. Each girl colors part of it red during her shift to show whether or not she's on target to make their goal. Poor Ari's probably gonna end up kissing a lot of frogs today for the sake of the school. If it helps to know…"

"Yes?" Gabe prompted, surprised to see Quinn blushing.

"Lilah and I asked her to work some of the shifts at the booth, but that was before…you."

Her words humbled him. He recalled too vividly how he'd hurt Arianne by making her think he wouldn't want anyone to know that they were a newly formed couple. Who had he been kidding? It was Mistletoe; people would figure it out. By not openly acknowledging his budding feelings for Arianne, he wasn't protecting her but merely fueling the potential for speculative gossip. He should be thrilled that people might link him and Arianne; she was certainly the best thing to happen to him in a long time.

"Quinn, you don't owe me any explanations. But thanks for thinking of me."

She shot him a mischievous smile. "Well, I just know how *I'd* feel if Patrick was over there working that particular booth. So I empathize."

He dropped an arm around her shoulder and squeezed in a quick, casual hug and thanked her again for the funnel cake.

"I promise to be back later with something to drink," she said. "But the cakes were too big for me to carry beverages, too!"

The festival committee had agreed ahead of time that the pirate plank fundraiser would only be open for certain posted hours since a lot of the officials who were being "dunked" also had other duties they had to perform while they were here. Gabe hung a sign that invited interested parties to come back in an hour, and used the break to check the platform stability and replace the dozen or so balls that had fallen out while victims were exiting the enclosure.

He was checking underneath the platform to see if any balls had rolled under there when there was a slight, raspy sound. A woman clearing her throat. He hopped up.

"We'll be open again in an— Mrs. Ortz?"

Looking distinctly uncomfortable, Earline Ortz stood, clutching her handbag and peering at him through horn-rimmed glasses. Even though they'd never spoken, seeing her gave him a macabre sense of déjà vu. In the weeks before he'd slept with Shay, he'd dreamed of her often; after her death, it became her parents' grief-stricken faces that haunted his nightmares.

He wanted to ask Mrs. Ortz what he could do for her,

but the answer was painfully obvious: nothing. She'd lost her only child, and he could never take back his part in that.

She cleared her throat a second time. "I'm working the crafts booth for the church," she said suddenly, as if to explain her appearance here.

The booth that was down on Poplar Street? It was three blocks away. He remained silent, knowing she'd sought him out for a reason, uncertain he wanted to know what that reason was.

She squared her slim shoulders. "Mr. Sloan, not a day goes by that I don't miss my daughter. I loved her very much."

He winced, wondering if there would ever come a time when the guilt left him completely. Rationally he knew that he was no more to blame than the Templetons, but it was hard to be rational about it when *they* were dead.

"I'm sure she loved you, too," he replied stiffly. He'd endured the looks on the Ortzs' faces when he passed them in town, endured being the occasional subject of gossip, had even endured being questioned by the police, but there had never been any direct confrontation. Was that why Earline was here now, to finally blame him face-to-face?

"But even though I loved Shay," Earline said, her voice cracking when she said her daughter's name, "I wasn't blind to her faults. Her father never wanted to see her as anything other than his little girl, but… Mr. Sloan, are you a churchgoing man?"

"Not regularly," he admitted.

"We talk about the power of forgiveness, even as we

cling to grudges and old hurts. Miss Waide was right in what she said this week. It's been fourteen years, and you shouldn't be punished forever. I... Between you and me, Mr. Sloan, I want you to know, I think it was a terrible accident involving people who'd made bad judgments in their personal life. I don't think— It wasn't your fault."

Gabe was appalled to find that his eyes stung. Unchecked emotion welled up in him. Not even his own father had ever absolved him of responsibility for Shay's death. If anything, Jeremy had implied that his adulterous son had reaped what he'd sown, the "wages of sin" being death. Gabe was overcome with the urge to hug Mrs. Ortz, but recognized that, in spite of her benevolence today, she probably wouldn't return his warm and fuzzy sentiments.

"Mrs. Ortz." There was a lump in his throat, and his choked voice sounded alien in his own ears. *"Thank you."*

She paused as if she might answer, then merely nodded and bustled away.

As the woman retreated down the path between buildings, Gabe looked around him. The sky seemed bluer, the birdsong seemed more harmonious. It was a new world.

No, the world's the same. It's a new you. And he knew exactly who had been responsible for most of the recent changes in his life. If not for what Arianne had said at the town hall, would Earline have been moved to make today's overture? For the first time in fourteen years, he felt like a free man, unshackled from shame and other people's censure.

I have to tell Ari.

He covered the distance that led to the kissing booth, then drew up short at the line. There were at least half a dozen paying customers in front of him. Gabe wanted to knock them all aside, take her into his arms and share with her his unbelievably good news.

Since the fair's patrons were good sports here for a bit of fun—he noticed many of the guys flirting with Arianne in bad piratespeak—they paid their dollar, dropped a quick kiss and went away. The line moved at a brisk clip. Ari, who was busy making change in the cash box and filling in tiny premarked sections of the lip poster, had yet to notice him. As he waited his turn with the woman he'd foolishly tried to walk away from, Gabe realized what he wanted to do.

He saw the exact moment she spotted him. She froze in the middle of teasing Beau Albright—the guy had made a joke about the size of his cannon, and Arianne had pretended disgust, calling him a bilge rat. Her eyes locked with Gabe's and even from this distance, the electric current between them was unmistakable.

Hell with this. I'm claiming what's mine. He reached into his pocket, slapped the patch over his eye and cut in line.

"Away wi' ye," he growled to the two guys who'd been ahead of him.

Arianne put a hand on her hip, projecting a fierce demeanor, but her lips twitched in amusement. And desire for him danced in her eyes. "And what d' ye think yer doing?"

Gabe slapped his dollar down on the cash box, then stepped behind the table.

"You know," she whispered, a sweet quaver in her voice as she melted against him, "you're not really supposed to be back here."

He grinned. "Pirates don't have to follow rules." Then he bent her backward over his arm and kissed her with fourteen years' worth of pent-up emotion, never wanting to come up for air, never wanting to return to the bleak world as it had been before Arianne. Distantly he was aware of applause and whistles.

Pulling away, he studied her face, hoping his stunt hadn't angered her.

She winked at him. "So does this mean you're okay with people knowing we're dating?"

"The more, the better."

Starting with all the guys behind him who'd been planning to kiss Gabe's girl. He reached into his wallet and extracted all the cash he had—two twenty-dollar bills.

Ari's eyes went wide. "Forty bucks?"

"Does that meet your shift quota?"

"Well, yeah, but—"

"Then I claim the pirate queen for my own," he informed the crowd.

Onlookers who hadn't expected to get nearly this much entertainment value hooted and stamped their feet in approval. Arianne squeaked in surprise when he hefted her into his arms and carried her away.

"I should apologize for my rash behavior," he told her,

with absolutely no intention of doing so. "But you know how it is when you get an impulse. You have to act on it."

"I can't believe I let you talk me into this," Gabe groused good-naturedly from the nursery doorway.

"As if you had better plans!" Arianne wasn't fooled by his bluster. He looked perfectly content to be here with her. And since she'd never spent this much time alone with a baby, she greatly appreciated the extra pair of hands. She'd canceled going to an annual Halloween bash one of her college friends threw, but she didn't mind.

"Do you even get trick-or-treaters out where you live?" she asked, trying to picture Gabe handing out mini candy bars to three-foot-tall princesses and goblins.

"No, which is my point. We could have had a completely uninterrupted Halloween evening." He waggled his eyebrows. "You could have busted out that lady pirate costume…."

She shot him a look as she finished dressing her niece. "As I recall, you ripped that pirate costume trying to get it off me last weekend."

"Ah, yes." He smiled in fond recollection. "Good times."

"Here, come take Bailey for me." The high-tech diaper pail was getting full, and Arianne needed a few minutes and two free hands to figure out how to empty it.

Gabe obliged, but held Bailey slightly away from his body, eyeing her as nervously as if she were a ticking bomb. Which in some ways, Arianne supposed, babies were.

Arianne laughed. "You're not scared, are you?"

"Scared of this beautiful girl?" He grinned at the infant, who cooed adoringly in return. "Of course not. What I'm scared of is dinner with your family next weekend."

The Waides often had Sunday dinner as a family, but this weekend was Rachel and David's first away from the baby. They'd gone to nearby Helen, Georgia, leaving Bailey in the care of her doting aunt. Arianne tried not to take it personally that they'd called eight times to check on the baby and had only been gone since that morning. When the family reconvened for their usual group meal next week, Gabe would be joining them.

"They'll love you," she promised, passing by him toward the garage. "But if you want any more pointers—"

"Enough with the pointers. I didn't study as hard for the SATs as you've been drilling me for this meal."

Was she really that bad? she wondered as she washed her hands. All she wanted was for everyone to see Gabe the way she did—warm and wonderful. He was coming out of his shell more, but it wasn't easy to overcome a decade of antisocial habits.

She joined them in the living room, where Gabe had set the baby on an activity blanket on the floor. "You know what I think would be fun?"

Gabe looked imploringly heavenward. "Please let there be costumes involved in this suggestion."

"Fetishist!" she scolded. "I was thinking about a book club."

"A book club?" he echoed, looking at her as if she'd suddenly started speaking Swahili.

"Yeah. You like to read, right? Why not get a group of our friends together, maybe every two weeks. We could decide what we wanted to read, then talk about the story—the themes, the symbols, what we liked, what we would have changed. My mom and dad belong to one and really enjoy it."

He'd gone from looking confused to looking the same way he had earlier when he'd smelled a dirty diaper. "I don't know, Ari. I like reading whatever I'm in the mood for when I have the time, not trying to meet someone else's deadline. Themes? Symbols? Half your friends are teachers."

"So?" She plopped down on the floor next to Bailey. "I thought you liked Quinn and Patrick and Lilah."

"I do. I just have…a different background."

She winced. Did he feel somehow inferior because he hadn't gone to college? She'd been trying to brainstorm ways to make him feel *more* included.

After the festival last weekend, they'd gone to her place and made love for hours. And then they'd talked for hours. Gabe hadn't abandoned his job search outside of Mistletoe. He'd told her candidly that he did want to be with her and that they could discuss their options as individual opportunities arose, but he wanted at least to investigate those possibilities instead of continuing to stagnate the way he'd allowed himself to for so long.

"You understand, don't you?" he'd asked.

Yes.

But understanding didn't quell that horrible sensation

she got in the pit of her stomach whenever she thought about him leaving. He had such potential here! People were just getting to know him. Arianne kept hoping that maybe if he strengthened his relationships in Mistletoe—maybe played softball with Nick or invited Patrick over for a video game showdown or double-dated with Lilah and Tanner at On Tap Friday nights…

She was a lousy girlfriend, she admitted to herself as she watched him play with the baby. What kind of loyal supporter helped you proofread résumés while at the same time secretly crossing her fingers that nobody would call you about a job?

Chapter Fifteen

Arianne had just parked her car Friday afternoon when her cell phone rang. "Hello?"

"Where are you?" Gabe asked, his tone jubilant.

"Outside the post office. I promised Mom I'd run in before they closed today and pick her up some stamps. Why?"

"Because I thought we might have dinner together and celebrate some minor news."

She leaned back in her seat, loving how happy he sounded. "I'm always up for a celebration. What's the news?"

"That college in South Carolina? They want to have a phone interview with me next week, and if that goes well, meet me in person. They also offer an internship program for employees who are interested in pursuing degrees."

"That's great." But the words of congratulations were like gravel in her mouth. Did he have to sound so overjoyed about getting away from here?

He tuned into her dismay immediately. "We'll figure something out. You know I don't want to stop seeing you."

"Neither do I." But seeing him would be more difficult if they were in two separate states.

It's not as if they were talking about a short-term assignment, where he went for a few quarters of college work and came back. Even as happy as he'd seemed during the week since the festival, he'd never talked about settling permanently in Mistletoe.

Arianne tried to imagine herself anywhere else and failed. This town was as much her family as David or Tanner. "You know," she said, "Mistletoe does have a really good community college."

"So you've mentioned. About a dozen times this week." He sighed, and she felt terrible, as if she'd sucked the wind from his sails. "It's almost five. If you're going to run into the post office, I should let you go."

"What about dinner?" *Nice going, Ari.* He'd been so upbeat when he called.

"You can call me back," he said tersely. Then he disconnected.

Arianne got out of the car, determined to get her reservations under control so that by the time she spoke to him again, she could sound genuinely congratulatory instead of resentful.

A man leaving the building with his mail held the door open for her, and she stopped in her tracks.

There was a reproachful look in his familiar silvery eyes. "You going in or not?" he asked.

"You!" It seemed like a sign from the heavens. "You're Gabe's father."

The man shifted uncomfortably as if uneasy with that designation. "I'm Jeremy Sloan."

Jeremy Sloan, the man who'd loved his dead wife more than the son who had lived. "I'm Arianne Waide, your son's girlfriend." Which made them like in-laws once removed, and Ari had never been shy about giving her relatives, even the distant ones, advice.

"I don't suppose you've ever considered making amends for being a bad father?" she snapped, angry that she might be losing Gabe just as she found him and frustrated with Jeremy's role in that. Perhaps if he and his son had mended their fences, Gabe could be more content here.

Jeremy's mouth dropped open, his face coloring. "Is that what he says, that I was a bad father?"

"He doesn't say much one way or the other," she admitted. "I was putting words in his mouth. But come on! When was the last time you spent any time with him? Do you know that even Earline Ortz spoke to him last weekend? *She* forgave him for Shay's death, so why can't you?"

"Ms. Waide, *my* relationship with *my* son is none of your business." He let go of the door and marched past her on the sidewalk.

Arianne took a breath, realizing she'd botched this conversation unforgivably, but she hadn't been prepared. "Mr. Sloan? I don't think you *have* a relationship with your son, and maybe you're okay with that. But if you aren't, act fast. He's leaving."

The man turned to face her. "Leaving? To go where? He's spent his whole life here."

"Be that as it may, he doesn't want to spend the *rest* of his life here," she said gently, pleased to see that Jeremy looked upset about this. Perhaps the threat of losing Gabe permanently would goad the man into action.

If Gabe really was moving soon, she'd like that to be her parting gift to him. He might think that all he needed for a fresh start was a new address, but you couldn't start anew if you were still emotionally chained to the old.

She just hoped that a new beginning for him didn't mean the end for them.

GABE WAS IN HELL. Oh, it might *look* like a charming Sunday dinner complete with smiling Waides and delicious homemade food—Ari hadn't exaggerated her mother's culinary prowess—but it was nonetheless Hades. Since Gabe had never had a serious romantic relationship before, he'd never had to Meet the Family before. It shouldn't be that hard, given that he already knew everyone seated around the table, but it was agonizing.

He was unused to anyone fussing over him, and Susan Waide's warm, maternal nature was making him vaguely uncomfortable. But at least she was better than Zachariah, who'd always considered Gabe one of his best clients and treated him well. Today the man was watching him intently beneath bushy eyebrows as if he knew exactly what Gabe and Arianne had been doing last night and emphatically did not approve. But the person at the table who was really driving him crazy was Arianne.

She'd been manic for the last couple of days, talking him up to people as if he were campaigning for an actual political position instead of the throwaway title of Mistletoe's Man of the Year. He was sure she meant for her enthusiastic praise to be flattering, yet she seemed almost condescending when he was sitting right there. As if she didn't trust him to speak for himself. She'd told her parents about the book he was reading and the jobs he'd done this week.

"Barb Echols told me at the grocery store that she just doesn't know what she would have done without Gabe," Arianne said. Then she turned and beamed at him as if she were a proud teacher and he was her most accomplished student.

The baby, who'd been sleeping in her bassinet in the next room, woke with a cry, and Rachel turned to ask her husband, "Will you go check on her? Please?"

"Or you could let Gabe do it." Arianne volunteered him. "You should have seen him last weekend. He was a natural. You'd think he was around babies every day!"

He glared. "Actually, if it's all the same to David, I was planning to finish my pork roast."

The truth was, while he'd had some fun moments playing with Bailey, he hadn't spent much time with babies and had found himself to be awkward and uncertain. Arianne knew that full well—she'd even called him on it. The way she was gushing now, embellishing the truth, made him feel as if she was overcompensating for some lack in his personality.

She'd told him repeatedly that if he made an effort with the people in this town, they'd like him. Apparently, if she didn't think *his* effort was enough, she'd start networking on his behalf. *I want a girlfriend, not a public relations agent!* It had been one thing for her to nominate him—against his will—for the Man of the Year title and extol his virtues then, but he wished she wouldn't lay it on so thick with her own family. Did she think he couldn't win them over on his own merits?

When Susan stood at the end of dinner and announced brightly that she was getting everyone's dessert—and that Arianne should come with her to help—Gabe wanted to cheer. The break would be nice. In fact, he was beginning to have a new appreciation for the merits of a long-distance relationship.

ARIANNE DUTIFULLY CROSSED to the cabinet and got out the dessert plates, but deep down she knew this wasn't why her mother had summoned her into the privacy of the kitchen.

"All right." Susan leaned against the kitchen island, making no move to slice the vanilla-glazed Bundt cake she'd made. "What is going on with you in there?"

Arianne pressed a hand to her forehead. "I know. I can't seem to shut up. I'm just…nervous."

"Get over it. I raised you to be a gracious hostess, and your guest looks like he's ready to throw himself into a ravine. Sweetheart, if *you* like him, we like him, so stop the hard sell. Petey Gruebner isn't this pushy when he's hocking used cars! Any moment now I expect you to tell us we have one year with zero interest, and that if we act now, we can get a second Gabe free."

Arianne didn't know whether to laugh at her mother or groan. "I'm really that bad?"

"Worse," her mother chirped. "And you're making everyone uncomfortable."

"I'll try to do better," she pledged. The truth was, her involuntary song and dance wasn't for her family's benefit. She knew they'd love Gabe—how could they not? No, it was *him* she was trying to impress.

She kept thinking that maybe if he felt important enough to the community here, loved enough, that he'd decide he wanted to stay. She just had to show him he belonged. An old song ran through her head: "Hold On Loosely." That's what she needed to do. She couldn't keep Gabe by clinging to him and thwarting his options for the future. But even knowing that, she had trouble adopting a *que sera* attitude. Every day she was with him, she fell a little further even though she would have sworn that wasn't possible. Apparently her love for Gabe was a bottomless pit.

"I'm taking this cake to the table," her mother informed her. "You, take a couple of deep breaths and get it together."

"Yes, ma'am."

When Ari returned to the dining room, she resolved to keep her mouth full of moist, rich dessert and shut the hell up before she did anything to alienate the guest of honor further. Luckily the mellowing properties of comfort food went a long way toward decreasing the stress level at the table.

Gabe seemed contentedly sated as he pushed his plate away. "That was fantastic, Susan." She'd pshawed his earlier attempts at calling her Mrs. Waide.

Lilah nodded enthusiastically. "I remember the first Thanksgiving I ever had here. The food was so amazing, I couldn't stop eating until I literally thought I was going to pop. And *then* she brought out the desserts. Lord knows how I managed to zip my Winter Wonderland formal dress that year."

Susan smiled and turned to Gabe. "Do you have plans for Thanksgiving?"

His expression was skittish, and Arianne cursed silently. Had she turned him off the idea of spending time with her family? Or worse, spending time with her?

"No, ma'am," Gabe was forced to admit. "No definite plans yet. Things are kind of up in the air for me right now."

"Well, if you find yourself at loose ends, you're always welcome here," Susan said.

"And don't feel bad if you show up at the last minute," David said. "She makes enough food for roughly forty people, so there will be plenty to go around."

Tanner checked his watch. "Lilah, if we want to make that movie, we should clear off a couple of these plates and get going."

She stood, gathering dishes and utensils. "Anyone want to go with us?"

"Sounds like fun," Arianne said. "What are you seeing? Maybe Gabe and I can join you."

He shook his head. "I have a very early start tomorrow, so you'll have to count me out."

Disappointed, Arianne wondered how much of his answer stemmed from needing sleep and how much of it came from her being so frenetic tonight.

Everyone helped pitch in to clear the table, then began their goodbyes. Lilah and Tanner took off for their movie, and Arianne and Gabe left soon after so that he could take her home and get some sleep. Rachel complained laughingly that she and David might still be there come morning because that's how long it seemed to take to gather up all of Bailey's paraphernalia.

David agreed. "I live in terror that one of these days we're going to be so busy checking to make sure we have the car seat, the stroller frame, the diaper bag, the pump, the binky, the toys and the bassinet that we're going to back out of the driveway and realize we left *her*."

Inside Gabe's truck, neither of them said much.

Halfway to her house, Arianne admitted to herself that probably the best thing to do was apologize. "I'm sorry if you had a horrible time," she said.

"It wasn't horrible. Your family's great," he said neutrally. "In spite of the 'I own a shotgun' vibe I occasionally got from your dad."

She laughed. "Fathers are required to look that way at their daughters' dates. Don't take it personally."

Gabe stopped at a red light, resting his arms on the

steering wheel. "I think that's the first real laugh I've heard from you all evening. Everything else seemed a bit…forced."

"I really am sorry," she reiterated. "I know I was a spaz—I just couldn't stop myself. I guess I've had guys over for meals and movie nights and board games with the family before, but I've never taken home anyone as special to me as you are."

He gifted her with a bone-melting smile as he turned onto her street. "Put that way, it's difficult to stay mad at you."

"Good! Because I'd hate for you to turn down my mom's Thanksgiving invitation just because I screwed up tonight." She stared out the window, troubled. "You really *don't* have plans?"

"No, why would I?"

Because he had a parent living in the same zip code! She knew they were estranged, but family—even family who didn't like each other—got together for the holidays. It was ritual. Similar to people who didn't actually belong to a church but still showed up somewhere for Easter service. She'd assumed from the way Gabe talked that he and his dad didn't spent the holidays together, but hearing it confirmed was different.

She glanced back at him. "David was serious when he said my mom makes enough food for forty. So you could invite your dad to come, too. If you wanted."

He slammed the truck into Park, the gears grinding discordantly. "If *I* wanted? What have I said or done that makes you think I want anything to do with that man?"

"But he's the only father you're ever going to have," she said philosophically.

"Look, I know this is difficult for you to understand since you come from such a close-knit family, but I'm fine not having a relationship with him."

"What if you aren't?" she pressed, thinking about the pain she'd seen in his face the night he told her about his mom's death. "What if he's subconsciously the reason you stayed in Mistletoe, because you hoped that somewhere down the road the two of you could—"

"I'm *not* staying in Mistletoe, remember? So it's a moot point. Look, Ari, if I'm here, I'll have Thanksgiving with you and your family, but I'm not spoiling the day by asking that man to join us, so just drop it. Even if I did invite him, he wouldn't come. He wants just as little to do with me as I do with him."

"I don't know." Sure, Jeremy Sloan had given her the cold shoulder the other day, but there'd been a sense of shocked loss in his expression after she told him Gabe was going away. Not that the intractable man had done anything about it! "When I talked to him—"

"You talked to my father? About me?" Gabe gripped the steering wheel tightly. Since they'd already arrived at their location, she couldn't help wondering if he was pretending it was her neck.

"I didn't call him at home or anything. I just happened to run into him out of the blue. It seemed like a good idea to—"

"You and I have very different opinions of what constitutes a good idea. You can't keep doing this!"

"Doing what?" she demanded, exasperated that he'd cut her off again. "Bumping into people at the post office?"

"No, trying to micromanage my life! I'm not some pet project."

That stung. She had Gabe's best interests at heart. She wanted him to be whole and happy and she believed he was deluding himself when he said making peace with his father wasn't part of that. "You know that's not how I see you," she said, opening her door.

"Do I? You appeared on the scene suddenly telling me what to do, trying to manipulate me into making changes."

"Damn good changes!" Even if he was being too stubborn to admit the truth. "I've made more improvements on your so-called life in four weeks than you have in fourteen years! And this is the thanks I get?"

He clenched his jaw. "I didn't ask for your interference, Arianne, and I don't want it."

She climbed out of the truck, so furious at the way he characterized her that she almost couldn't speak. A manipulative control freak? Is that how he saw her? Her initial impression of Gabe had been that he wasn't in the right emotional place for a relationship, and now she suspected she'd been correct. He wasn't used to sharing his life with anyone else. Would he ever value her input, her attempts to demonstrate how much she cared about him, or was she simply making them both crazy?

She needed to stop clinging to the idea of what they could have together and simply let him be. "The good news is, you won't have to worry about my 'interference' anymore. And don't trouble yourself over the logistics of a long-distance relationship. A clean break is probably best for everyone."

This time, she wasn't going to wait for *him* to walk away.

Chapter Sixteen

Gabe's week passed with agonizing slowness, each day dragging into the next. Even the would-be bright spot of his great phone interview dimmed when he realized he wanted to share the news with Arianne. Unfortunately she wasn't speaking to him.

He toyed with the notion of apologizing to her, convinced enough of her feelings for him that he suspected he could get her to give him another chance. But why? It was an ugly pattern in their relationship, his capitulating. She'd tried to bully him, albeit charmingly, into volunteering for the fall festival and it certainly hadn't been his idea to participate in this Man of the Year nonsense. If you gave Arianne an inch, she didn't just take a mile, she built a freaking highway. *Right through my life.*

Sure, he missed her now, but once the initial pangs had passed, he'd realize that it was better this way. He didn't want the stress of arguing with her, of fighting to maintain the right to make his own adult decisions. In a few weeks, he'd get over her and his life could calm down again.

But now, with the possibility of running into her around every corner, he was more eager than ever to get out of Mistletoe. Even seeing her brothers was a painful reminder.

When Tanner saw Gabe seated alone at the Dixieland Diner, the man took it upon himself to drop into the booth. "You look like hell, Sloan."

What was it with the uninvited Waides and their unsolicited opinions?

"Coincidentally enough, my sister's had that same expression for the past four days," Tanner added.

I don't want to hear about Arianne. "We're not seeing each other anymore."

"Yeah, I got that."

"If you sat down to read me the riot act over the breakup, you should know that she was the one who—"

"No riot act," Tanner assured him. "I love Arianne, but God help the man she ends up with. She's a lot to take."

Gabe had to bite his tongue to keep from defending her.

"I can understand why you decided it wasn't working out," Tanner added, "but it's a onetime decision. Now that you've realized you're not a good fit for each other, stay away from her. Because if you come back and break her heart, David and I are obligated as her brothers to break your legs."

As Gabe made the drive to South Carolina for his face-to-face interview, he realized that tonight was the town vote where the Mistletoe Man of the Year would be selected. He found himself irrationally grateful that he'd be in another state at the time. Not that he cared about the title—he'd abdicate to someone else in the unlikely event that he won—but he didn't like the embarrassment of a glaring loss, either.

Arianne was clearly insane if she thought people would choose him over Nick Zeth, a fireman considered good-looking and lovable; or Dylan Echols, who had played for the Atlanta Braves and was considered a celebrity in Mistletoe! *And she called me deluded?* Why couldn't she accept that just because she believed in him, she couldn't force her opinion on other people?

Probably because she was so accustomed to getting her way.

But he felt ashamed of the barbed thought as soon as he'd entertained it. Whatever her character flaws, she had believed in him. How many people could he say that about in his life?

"Crap!" Belatedly realizing that he'd missed his exit, Gabe prepared to turn the truck around and turned up his radio to drown out thoughts about Arianne Waide.

But she crept back into his mind anyway. When he parked his truck in front of the administrative building he was supposed to report to, he could almost hear her wishing him luck. *You can do it!* Go away, he told the phantom cheerleader, irrationally annoyed with her perky attitude. *You didn't even want me to get the job.*

True, but she'd gone through his closet anyway and told him which ties made him look sharp and what outfits just made him look as if he was trying too hard. And she'd helped him refine his résumé. She was a lot like her mother, a nurturer. He suspected that Susan Waide wasn't shy about giving advice to her children and husband, just as he suspected that advice was often right.

Had Gabe found Arianne's meddling more overbearing than it really was simply because he wasn't used to anyone caring enough about him to interfere?

Disturbed by the possibility that he'd judged her too harshly, he entered the building and told himself to focus. This interview could mean a fresh start and a new life for him. Maybe even work put toward a college degree. *Get your head on straight.*

But Arianne was too deeply entrenched in his thoughts for him to ignore. When the interviewer discussed a traditional campus festival they held in the spring, all Gabe could think about was Arianne in her pirate costume. And out of it. When Gabe saw the desktop picture of the man's wife and child, he couldn't help recalling the way Arianne looked holding Bailey. *She'll make a great mom.*

She'd be fiercely protective, and he imagined that any child of hers would sometimes chafe under Arianne's insistence that she knew best, but that child would also grow up secure in the knowledge that he or she was unconditionally loved.

Gabe had spent the better part of the interview so distracted that he was almost startled when it ended.

"I think that's all the questions we have for you," the man behind the desk said genially. "Unless you have any more for us, I'll let Bruce show you around the grounds some. While the hiring committee writes up their applicant recommendation, you be thinking about whether or not, if offered the job, you could see making a home here at Whisthaven."

Home. The word was a revelation. He'd felt torn recently, trying to decide if the right home for him was Mistletoe or somewhere else. But home wasn't a place. It was a state of being—a sense of belonging, of knowing you were loved even if the people who loved you aggravated the hell out of you, a sense of security and the knowledge that someone else had your back, even while you argued that you could take care of yourself.

Home was Arianne.

WAIDE SUPPLY WAS JUST opening for the day when Gabe strode through the doors. After a long drive back to Mistletoe, which had given him too much time to think about what he'd lost, he'd spent a sleepless night staring at his clock and waiting for this moment. Out of sheer impulse, he'd even reached once for his phone, but sanity had prevailed. If you woke a woman up at three in the morning, she was probably even less inclined to take you back. Gabe was already at enough of a disadvantage.

Arianne was setting up an end-cap display, while her father and David stood looking at some kind of paperwork at the counter. Gabe made a beeline for her, fully aware that the two Waide men had both stilled and were watching him.

David stepped forward, inserting himself between Gabe and Ari. He flashed a shark's toothy smile. "Anything I can help you with this morning?"

Arianne got to her feet, looking tiny in comparison to her brother. It was funny, Gabe had noticed her height early on, but after a while, her larger-than-life personality made her seem a lot taller than she was.

He looked over David's shoulder, appealing to her directly. "Can I talk to you?"

She jerked her thumb toward an open box that contained many smaller boxes of nails. "As you can see, I'm busy laying out the sales inventory."

"I can help," he said, probably sounding desperate and not really caring.

Her eyes flashed at him. "Teamwork isn't really your thing, is it, Gabe? I pegged you more as someone who worked alone."

"Maybe that's just because it's what I was used to. Maybe it took me longer than most to recognize a good thing when I had it."

She bit her lip, looking beautiful and vulnerable, and Gabe considered removing David bodily from his path so that he could go hug her.

David raised an eyebrow, shooting pointed glances at Gabe's kneecaps. "Didn't you and Tanner have a discussion a few days ago?" he asked meaningfully. "Maybe your being here isn't such a good idea."

"It's probably the best idea I've ever had," Gabe countered.

Arianne had narrowed her eyes at her brother. "What do you mean, he and Tanner had a discussion? Do you two not understand that I'm a big girl now? I can take care of myself."

Gabe couldn't help it, he threw his head back and laughed. Both Waide siblings looked at him. He ignored David altogether and locked eyes with Arianne. "You can't have it both ways, sweetheart. Is it the right of a loved one to interfere, or should they stay out of your private life and let you make your own choices?"

She fought a smile, sighing in resignation. "Damn. I hate it when other people are right. Dad, David, could we have a minute?"

Zachariah looked unconvinced, but David led their father away.

"Thank you," Gabe said. "I would have said it in front of them if I had to, but this is better. Arianne, I love you."

She pressed a hand to her abdomen, looking stunned by the bald admission. "But I'm bossy and interfering and too stubborn for my own good. I'll drive you crazy."

"I'll learn to live with it," he vowed. "Just like you have to learn to live with me withdrawing and being moody and needing time to adjust to an idea before I can embrace it as fully as you can."

"I don't know." She plopped right down on the floor as if she were too drained to stand, and leaned against a shelving unit. "I feel like someone used my heart as a Ping-Pong ball, and I'm not sure I'm cut out for any more of that. A long-distance relationship—"

"Won't be an issue. You were right when you said I like to work alone. I set my own hours, I don't have to put up with an obnoxious boss, and I've already established a solid client base. I don't think I have the patience to start over somewhere new at the bottom. I can be happy in Mistletoe…as long as I'm with you."

"You're sure I'm what you want?" she asked in a small voice.

He slid down next to her, taking her hands in his. "I know I said some hurtful things to you. I was angry, and you were pushing all the wrong buttons. I doubt it will be the last fight we have. But give me a chance to get better at this. I want to redeem myself."

Actually, it was Arianne and her stubborn caring that had already redeemed him. He wasn't the same man he was a month ago, and he was glad for that.

The happiness spread inside, until he felt lit up with it. He grinned at her. "You *have* to take me back. I won't take no for an answer. I'll follow you to your favorite restaurants, I'll call you on the phone, I'll nominate you for bizarre local honors…"

She beamed at him unabashedly. "Now what kind of psycho with no sense of personal boundaries would do all that?"

"The kind I love," he said against her lips.

"I love you, too." And then she kissed him.

He'd been right—it was exactly like coming home.

Epilogue

I cannot believe I'm up here. Gabe felt a bit foolish sitting on the back of the convertible and waving to all and sundry. It truly was a testament to how much Arianne could talk him into—not that he minded completely. He especially liked her inventive ways of trying to cajole him into a good mood first.

At the end of the parade, people shook his hand and clapped him on the back, all wishing him a Happy Thanksgiving. Gabe acknowledged them politely, but was trying to find the short love of his life in the crowd. He was so focused on that that it took him a moment to realize that the person in his path was his father.

"Dad." Gabe froze. "You come to the parade?"

Jeremy Sloan looked away. "Not every year. So you're Man of the Year, huh?"

"Seems that way," Gabe said, feeling painfully embarrassed. His father probably thought the whole thing was stupid.

Jeremy grunted. "Your mother would have loved that."

Gabe was stunned, but not sure how to respond. Thank you?

"Well, have a nice Thanksgiving."

"You, too." Watching his dad go, Gabe almost called him back to ask whether he had plans for dinner. But he couldn't quite voice the question. Not yet, maybe someday soon.

"Just for the record, I want you to take note of my standing here and *not* offering you any advice whatsoever," came a voice from behind him. "Even though it's killing me."

"Ari." He spun around with a smile. "I was looking for you."

"I was stuck in line at the concessions booth. You seemed sort of good-naturedly miserable during the parade and I thought this might cheer you up." She held up a waffle cone loaded with two scoops of chocolate.

"Ice cream!" He bent to kiss the woman who understood him so well—and loved him anyway. "My hero."

* * * * *

*Celebrate 60 years of pure reading pleasure
with Harlequin®!*

To commemorate the event, Silhouette Special Edition invites you to Ashley O'Ballivan's bed-and-breakfast in the small town of Stone Creek. The beautiful innkeeper will have her hands full caring for her old flame Jack McCall. He's on the run and recovering from a mysterious illness, but that won't stop him from trying to win Ashley back.

*Enjoy an exclusive glimpse of Linda Lael Miller's
AT HOME IN STONE CREEK
Available in November 2009 from
Silhouette Special Edition®*

The helicopter swung abruptly sideways in a dizzying arch, setting Jack McCall's fever-ravaged brain spinning.

His friend's voice sounded tinny, coming through the earphones. "You belong in a hospital," he said. "Not some backwater bed-and-breakfast."

All Jack really knew about the virus raging through his system was that it wasn't contagious, and there was no known treatment for it besides a lot of rest and quiet. "I don't like hospitals," he responded, hoping he sounded like his normal self. "They're full of sick people."

Vince Griffin chuckled but it was a dry sound, rough at the edges. "What's in Stone Creek, Arizona?" he asked. "Besides a whole lot of nothin'?"

Ashley O'Ballivan was in Stone Creek, and she was a whole lot of somethin', but Jack had neither the strength nor the inclination to explain. After the way he'd ducked out six months before, he didn't expect a welcome, knew he didn't deserve one. But Ashley, being Ashley, would take him in whatever her misgivings.

He had to get to Ashley; he'd be all right.

He closed his eyes, letting the fever swallow him.

There was no telling how much time had passed when he became aware of the chopper blades slowing overhead. Dimly, he saw the private ambulance waiting on the airfield outside of Stone Creek; it seemed that twilight had descended.

Jack sighed with relief. His clothes felt clammy against his flesh. His teeth began to chatter as two figures unloaded a gurney from the back of the ambulance and waited for the blades to stop.

"Great," Vince remarked, unsnapping his seat belt. "Those two look like volunteers, not real EMTs."

The chopper bounced sickeningly on its runners, and Vince, with a shake of his head, pushed open his door and jumped to the ground, head down.

Jack waited, wondering if he'd be able to stand on his own. After fumbling unsuccessfully with the buckle on his seat belt, he decided not.

When it was safe the EMTs approached, following Vince, who opened Jack's door.

His old friend Tanner Quinn stepped around Vince, his grin not quite reaching his eyes.

"You look like hell warmed over," he told Jack cheerfully.

"Since when are you an EMT?" Jack retorted.

Tanner reached in, wedged a shoulder under Jack's right arm and hauled him out of the chopper. His knees immediately buckled, and Vince stepped up, supporting him on the other side.

"In a place like Stone Creek," Tanner replied, "everybody helps out."

They reached the wheeled gurney, and Jack found himself on his back.

Tanner and the second man strapped him down, a process that brought back a few bad memories.

"Is there even a hospital in this place?" Vince asked irritably from somewhere in the night.

"There's a pretty good clinic over in Indian Rock," Tanner answered easily, "and it isn't far to Flagstaff." He paused to help his buddy hoist Jack and the gurney into the back of the ambulance. "You're in good hands, Jack. My wife is the best veterinarian in the state."

Jack laughed raggedly at that.

Vince muttered a curse.

Tanner climbed into the back beside him, perched on some kind of fold-down seat. The other man shut the doors.

"You in any pain?" Tanner said as his partner climbed into the driver's seat and started the engine.

"No." Jack looked up at his oldest and closest friend and wished he'd listened to Vince. Ever since he'd come down with the virus—a week after snatching a five-year-old girl back from her non-custodial parent, a small-time Colombian drug dealer—he hadn't been able to think about anyone or anything but Ashley. When he *could* think, anyway.

Now, in one of the first clearheaded moments he'd experienced since checking himself out of Bethesda the day before, he realized he might be making a major mistake. Not by facing Ashley—he owed her that much and a lot more. No, he could be putting her in danger, putting Tanner and his daughter and his pregnant wife in danger, too.

"I shouldn't have come here," he said, keeping his voice low.

Tanner shook his head, his jaw clamped down hard as though he was irritated by Jack's statement.

"This is where you belong," Tanner insisted. "If you'd had sense enough to know that six months ago, old buddy, when you bailed on Ashley without so much as a fare-thee-well, you wouldn't be in this mess."

Ashley. The name had run through his mind a million times in those six months, but hearing somebody say it out loud was like having a fist close around his insides and squeeze hard.

Jack couldn't speak.

Tanner didn't press for further conversation.

The ambulance bumped over country roads, finally hitting smooth blacktop.

"Here we are," Tanner said. "Ashley's place."

* * * * *

Will Jack be able to patch things up with Ashley,
or will his past put the woman he loves
in harm's way?
Find out in
AT HOME IN STONE CREEK
by Linda Lael Miller
Available November 2009 from
Silhouette Special Edition®

This November,
Silhouette Special Edition®
brings you

NEW YORK TIMES
BESTSELLING AUTHOR

LINDA LAEL
MILLER

At Home in
Stone Creek

Available in November
wherever books are sold.

SSELLM60BPA

HARLEQUIN

Ambassadors

Want to share your passion for reading Harlequin® Books?

Become a Harlequin Ambassador!

Harlequin Ambassadors are a group of passionate and well-connected readers who are willing to share their joy of reading Harlequin® books with family and friends.

You'll be sent all the tools you need to spark great conversation, including free books!

All we ask is that you share the romance with your friends and family!

You'll also be invited to have a say in new book ideas and exchange opinions with women just like you!

To see if you qualify* to be a Harlequin Ambassador, please visit www.HarlequinAmbassadors.com.

*Please note that not everyone who applies to be a Harlequin Ambassador will qualify. For more information please visit www.HarlequinAmbassadors.com.

Thank you for your participation.

BAP09BPA

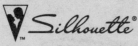

Romantic
SUSPENSE

**Sparked by Danger,
Fueled by Passion.**

*Blackout
At Christmas*

Beth Cornelison,
Sharron McClellan,
Jennifer Morey

What happens when a major blackout shuts
down the entire Western seaboard on Christmas
Eve? Follow stories of danger, intrigue and
romance as three women learn to trust their
instincts to survive and open their hearts to the
love that unexpectedly comes their way.

**Available November
wherever books are sold.**

Visit Silhouette Books at www.eHarlequin.com

SRS27653

HARLEQUIN® *Romance*®

This November,
queen of the rugged rancher

PATRICIA
THAYER

teams up with

DONNA ALWARD

to bring you an extra-special treat
this holiday season—

two romantic stories
in one book!

Join sisters Amelia and Kelley for Christmas at
Rocking H Ranch where these feisty cowgirls swap
presents for proposals, mistletoe for marriage and
experience the unbeatable rush of falling in love!

Available in November wherever books are sold.

REQUEST YOUR FREE BOOKS!
2 FREE NOVELS PLUS 2 FREE GIFTS!

HARLEQUIN®

American Romance®

Love, Home & Happiness!

YES! Please send me 2 FREE Harlequin® American Romance® novels and my 2 FREE gifts (gifts are worth about $10). After receiving them, if I don't wish to receive any more books, I can return the shipping statement marked "cancel." If I don't cancel, I will receive 4 brand-new novels every month and be billed just $4.24 per book in the U.S. or $4.99 per book in Canada.* That's a savings of close to 15% off the cover price! It's quite a bargain! Shipping and handling is just 50¢ per book. I understand that accepting the 2 free books and gifts places me under no obligation to buy anything. I can always return a shipment and cancel at any time. Even if I never buy another book from Harlequin, the two free books and gifts are mine to keep forever.

154 HDN E4DS   354 HDN E4D4

Name _____ (PLEASE PRINT) _____

Address _____ Apt. # _____

City _____ State/Prov. _____ Zip/Postal Code _____

Signature (if under 18, a parent or guardian must sign)

Mail to the **Harlequin Reader Service:**
IN U.S.A.: P.O. Box 1867, Buffalo, NY 14240-1867
IN CANADA: P.O. Box 609, Fort Erie, Ontario L2A 5X3

Not valid to current subscribers of Harlequin® American Romance® books.

Want to try two free books from another line?
Call 1-800-873-8635 or visit www.morefreebooks.com.

* Terms and prices subject to change without notice. Prices do not include applicable taxes. N.Y. residents add applicable sales tax. Canadian residents will be charged applicable provincial taxes and GST. Offer not valid in Quebec. This offer is limited to one order per household. All orders subject to approval. Credit or debit balances in a customer's account(s) may be offset by any other outstanding balance owed by or to the customer. Please allow 4 to 6 weeks for delivery. Offer available while quantities last.

Your Privacy: Harlequin is committed to protecting your privacy. Our Privacy Policy is available online at www.eHarlequin.com or upon request from the Reader Service. From time to time we make our lists of customers available to reputable third parties who may have a product or service of interest to you. If you would prefer we not share your name and address, please check here. ☐

HAR09R2

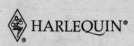